THUNDER IN MONTANA

When Mike Langton and his friends decide to settle and farm in Montana, they find tolerance and understanding from Zeke Hedley, but conflict from other cattlemen determined to keep an open range. Attempts to run the nesters out of the territory, to throw Hedley against Langton, result in beatings, arson, rustling and attempted rape, as rough justice is meted out.

Books by Jim Bowden
in the Linford Western Library:

SHOWDOWN IN SALT FORK
CAP

JIM BOWDEN

THUNDER IN MONTANA

Complete and Unabridged

931603

LINFORD
Leicester

First published in Great Britain in 1973

First Linford Edition
published July 1993

British Library CIP Data

Bowden, Jim
  Thunder in Montana.—Large print ed.—
Linford western library
I. Title II. Series
823.914 [F]

ISBN 0–7089–7369–8

Published by
F. A. Thorpe (Publishing) Ltd.
Anstey, Leicestershire
Set by Words & Graphics Ltd.
Anstey, Leicestershire
Printed and bound in Great Britain by
T. J. Press (Padstow) Ltd., Padstow, Cornwall

This book is printed on acid-free paper

1

"**N**ESTERS!"

The word hissed from Jake Thompson's thin lips as he topped the rise and automatically checked his horse in surprise at the sight of four men fixing barbed wire to a row of stakes stretching in a line across the hillside half-way down the slope.

Two other men were driving more stakes into the grassland, forming another line at right angles and crossing the stream which twisted through the hollow. Four wagons were drawn alongside the stream and four women were busy preparing a meal.

"We'll teach that crew," snapped Jake, his dark eyes smouldering in their sunken sockets as they swept across the scene. "Come on, Curly."

"Hold it," rapped Curly as Jake

started to move. "There's six of them. Reckon we'd better ride back to the Running W and inform the boss."

Jake's lean frame stiffened; his thin, gaunt face showed his contempt as he stared at Curly. "Yella, Curly?"

The stocky, broad-shouldered cowboy met Jake's gaze, his very being bristling at the taunt. Jake laughed at Curly's reaction. "You ride back if you want to but you know the boss, he'd expect you to do something. Besides there's no nester a match for our breed. Come on." He sent his horse down the hill and, after a moment's hesitation, Curly followed.

Discretion told him it was the wrong thing to do but he could not let Jake go alone. Common sense showed that it was better to collect a bunch of Running W riders and really impress the nesters, but he knew Jake wanted the glory.

The horses were half-way to the wire before the four men heard them. They looked up and, seeing the two cowboys, three of them glanced nervously at each other. The fourth kept staring at the riders, his sharp blue eyes taking in everything about the approaching men and he was quick to realize there was trouble. His lips tightened, his rugged, weather-beaten features took on a look of determination and his angular jaw seemed to jut that bit more.

Without looking at his companions he spoke decisively. "Spread out, don't bunch."

"Don't look for trouble, Mike," said one of the men.

"I won't, Tom, but I figure they will," returned Mike.

"Maybe we'd better move on," put in one of the others.

"Not this time, Will," replied Mike, his voice revealing his determination. "We've been through all this before. We said this would be the last time."

No one replied. They knew Mike was right. There had to be a final stopping, there had to be a time for no more moving, a time for final settlement no matter what the cost, a time to stand against the ranchers, to exert one's rights and be prepared to fight for them, otherwise a man lost faith with himself as well as with others and he was no longer a man.

They moved away from each other, arcing themselves from Mike. They heard the thud of the mallet stop and knew their two companions farther down the slope had seen the cowboys. The chattering which had drifted from the direction of the wagons was no longer there, and they knew the alarm their womenfolk would be feeling.

Jake pulled his horse to a halt four yards in front of Mike, while Curly stopped a few feet behind Jake and to his left. Jake noted that the nesters had spread out; they would be more awkward to deal with but they had not picked up their guns. Maybe they weren't looking for trouble and would move on after his warning.

Before Jake could speak Mike moved forward quickly to come close to the horse. "Howdy," he greeted with a friendly smile. "I'm Mike Langton." Jake ignored the proffered hand but Mike went on quickly trying to ease the tension that was there. "That's Tom Byrom, Will King, and the kid's Jamie Masters, and that's Ben Price and Mart Simpson just joining us."

The men nodded as Jake's glance passed over them. They sensed hostility from him whereas his companion's more open face showed less tension. Jake looked down on Mike, his eyes cold.

"Better pack up an' git movin'," he said.

Mike met his gaze. "Why?"

"This Running W land."

"Didn't see any fences when we got here, figured it was open range, anybody's for the taking."

"Wal, you figured wrong, so git movin'."

Mike shook his head. "It's you that's wrong."

Jake stiffened. His right hand moved

almost imperceptibly nearer his Colt. "You'd better . . . "

"You boss of the Running W?" cut in Mike.

"No," snapped Jake. "But that makes no difference."

"I figure it does. You've no right to move us. I'll talk to your boss but I reckon he has no right either. He'll have taken open range as his right, well the days of open range are over, barbed wire's seen to that. It's happened in other places and so Montana had better get used to it. I don't see any wire fences around here so I figure we've every right to put one up around our land."

"Your land!" Jake exploded.

"Your boss ain't got a fence round it so it's not his," put in Mike firmly.

"You're takin' good grazin' an' fencin' off some water, you can't come . . . "

"Can and will," cut in Mike sharply.

Jake's eyes flashed angrily at the nester's obstinacy.

"Are you movin'?"

"No, and you can't make us. We're here by right."

"This says I can!" snapped Jake. His hand snaked on to his Colt, but before the gun cleared leather, he felt a vice-like grip on his wrist.

As Mike's powerful grip closed on Jake, he jerked hard, bringing the cowboy crashing to the ground. Mike did not give him a chance to recover but was on him in a flash driving his fist into his face.

When Curly saw Jake pulled from the saddle his hand flashed to his Colt but Ben was quicker. The piece of wood which he had carried up the hillside now flew quickly and accurately taking Curly in the face. Curly lost his balance and before he could regain it the nesters were dragging him from the saddle. He was disarmed and held in a firm grip.

Mike dragged Jake to his feet and, pulling the cowboy's Colt from its holster, flung it away.

"Now, want to turn us off what's ours?" snarled Mike facing a dazed Jake.

A trickle of blood ran from Jake's lips. He wiped his hand across them then suddenly lunged at Mike. Poised, balanced on the balls of his feet, Mike stepped quickly to one side, avoiding Jake's attack, and drove his fist into Jake's face. Jake spun round. In spite of his thinness he was tough and wiry. It seemed as if he was up again before he touched the ground. He took Mike completely by surprise and threw the full weight of his body into his charge. They staggered back, locked together, for a few yards but as they hit the ground Jake twisted and was quickly on his feet. He spun round facing Mike. His eyes were fiery, burning with hate as he lunged again, lashing his foot into Mike's midriff as the nester was struggling to his feet. Mike yelled with the pain searing through his body as he fell backwards writhing on the ground.

8

With a yell of triumph Jake leaped towards his gun but Tom and Will had already moved and as Jake's fingers closed round the Colt a foot stamped hard on them. Jake yelled with the pain and was sent headlong to the ground with a crashing blow on the top of his back. He was dragged to his feet by two strong pairs of hands, his right hand limp as he still winced with the pain.

Hatred smouldered and flared as he was held between Tom and Will, and, although suffering, he gained some pleasure from seeing Mike dragging himself slowly to his feet holding his stomach. Curly struggled but was restrained firmly by Ben and Mart. Jamie was quickly beside Mike helping him up.

"You all right, Mike?" he asked.

Mike nodded, still gasping for breath. He held on to Jamie for a few moments then stretched himself. He winced and rubbed his stomach, then glared at Jake, anger rising in him. These cowpokes would have to be taught a lesson, a lesson which would impress their boss and make him see that the newcomers meant business, meant to stay on the land they were fencing, land they would farm and turn into a place to live. He was tired of moving on, tired of knuckling under to ranchers who always wielded more persuasive power. Now that was all going to be over. He had moved into Montana with friends equally determined to stay but Mike knew that determination needed bolstering up, they needed a leader to stand up to the ranchers. He realized if they had that they would back him all the way. They had found the land they wanted and nothing was going to make them move, Mike was determined on that.

He moved forward slowly, each step measured and menacing. Jake, seeing the hurt turn to hate in Mike's eyes, struggled to free himself but to no avail.

Mike reached the group, paused for a moment and then drove his fist hard into Jake's stomach. The cowboy gasped as the breath drove from his body. He started to double up but a fist crashed into his face jerking him upwards. Tom and Will held Jake firm and he cried out when Mike pounded him viciously in the stomach again. He hardly had time to feel the pain when more seared through his head as it was jerked sharply from side to side by Mike's huge hands. Blood spurted from a gash in his cheek, and ran from his torn lips. His left eye closed rapidly and his prominent eyebrows soon lacerated with the tearing blows.

"Mike! Mike! Steady on Mike!"

The voice sounded far away as Jake felt himself go limp in Tom and Will's grip. His brain reeled under the pounding.

Mike heard the distant voice calling him, but his mind was on the hated cowboy in front of him. He felt a hand on his arm. "Mike! That's enough!" It was eighteen-year-old Jamie's voice protesting in defence of a cowpoke.

Mike shook the hand from his arm. He swung round viciously, his eyes blazing.

"Keep out of it, Jamie, we're teaching these damned cowpokes a lesson the ranchers will take to heart." He swung the back of his hand hard across Jake's face. "They'll leave us alone after this."

"Mike! Mike! Don't! Please no more!"

The higher pitch of the voice penetrated Mike's mind. He hesitated in the middle of the next blow. Jamie felt relief. He turned and saw his sister hurrying up the hillside, half running, half stumbling in a desperate effort to reach the men grouped on the hillside. Her round, pink-cheeked face wore a look of anguish, her eyes reflected horror and a desire for the beating to stop.

"Mike! Mike! No! Don't!" The voice was there again driving into his brain. Mike dropped his arm. He stared about him, then back at the blood-spattered

12

figure in front of him. He rubbed his hand across his eyes, and shook his head. He had not realized how far he had gone. His mind had gone wild, driven almost beyond its limits in a desire to show the ranchers that this time Mike Langton was not going to move.

The young woman was beside them, grabbing at Mike's arms, pinning them to his side. "Please, Mike, no more," she looked up pleadingly into his face, her eyes full of love, not wanting to see her husband turning himself into an animal.

Mike sighed deeply as he looked deep into his wife's eyes. "Thank goodness you shouted, Jennie. I didn't know what I was doing, I'd have gone too far. Now please go back and let us finish what we started to do. It's all right," he added, to reassure her when he saw the concern on her face. He glanced at Jamie. "Take Jennie back please."

Jennie let go of Mike's arms and

Jamie helped her down the slope.

Mike looked back at Jake. He had meant to make an example of him, a warning to the ranchers, but in his almost beserk state of mind he had done more than he had originally intended. To make an example was one thing but to beat him into unconsciousness was another.

"All right, put him over the saddle." Tom and Will carried the cowboy to his horse and flung him face downwards across the saddle.

Mike walked across to Curly. "Take him back and tell your boss we're here to stay."

Words sprang to Curly's lips but he said nothing; he knew it would be useless. He shook himself free of Ben and Mart and started for his horse, but Mike grasped him by the arm.

"Don't forget to tell your boss I offered my hand of friendship but it was refused."

Curly said nothing, mounted his horse, gathered Jake's reins and sent the two animals up the slope, knowing full well what his boss's answer would be.

2

ONCE he had climbed the hillside Curly put the horses to the fastest pace he dare, considering the battered and unconscious Jake who lay across the saddle.

If only Jake had listened he wouldn't have suffered and no doubt a show of strength would have made the nesters think twice about staying. Now there would be trouble, big trouble; Al Barton was not the type of boss to see one of his men beaten up and do nothing about it, especially when a nester was the culprit.

At fifty-six, Al saw a way of life he had known for thirty years threatened by the arrival of nesters. He saw the open range, grazed by his large herds, under the threat of barbed wire and he wasn't going to sit idly by and watch the range carved up. He had heard how

16

serious this threat was farther east but as yet the few nesters who had drifted into this part of Montana had moved on, not wanting trouble at the hands of the cattlemen. But Al always said that one day a challenge would come, and as Curly rode back to the Running W he knew that time had come.

Luke Jennings, the Running W foreman, was first to spot Curly as he rode past the pole fence of the first corral. Calling to some of the other hands, Luke, fearing the worst when he saw the inert form lying across the saddle, ran to meet Curly.

"What happened?" he asked when he reached the horses. Shocked by the sight of Jake, his face was grim as he put the question.

"Nesters," replied Curly. "Out at Sioux Hollow."

Questions poured from other cowboys as they fell in beside Curly and walked back to the bunk-house. By the time Curly halted the horses they had the gist of the story and their anger was boiling at the treatment of one of their own kind by nesters.

Eager hands were lifting Jake gently from his horse by the time Al Barton, who had seen the arrival from the ranch-house, reached the group.

"All right, simmer down." Al's voice boomed. He was a big man, broad-set but with a fatness covering the once athletic frame. His presence spoke of authority, of a man who would stand no nonsense and who expected to be listened to. His broad powerful hands were gentle as he examined Jake's face. Behind the concern, which showed in his deep brown eyes, was a look which bore ill for the person who had dared to do this to one of his men.

"All right," he said, "take him inside. Gentle now. Blackie, get the doc." The orders came crisp and sharp. He looked over towards the ranch-house where his wife was standing on the verandah. "Meg! Meg!" he shouted. "Come over here."

Meg knew what it meant, someone

was hurt. She had tended injuries many times during their life at the Running W but, when she reached the bunk-house and the men parted to let her get at Jake, she recoiled momentarily at the sight of his battered face. But she was hardened by thirty years of life amongst men in the rough world of ranching, of having to tend to them in emergencies.

"Sorry, Meg." Al apologized for having to bring her. "I've sent for the doc."

Meg smiled wanly, "Good." She was already examining the injuries. Al was a rough, hard man, a strict, no nonsense man who made all the decisions but who had a gentler side which few people knew.

"Saddle up everyone, we've a call to make," ordered Al. The men started towards the door eager to have revenge for Jake's beating. "Not you, Hank." Al's fingers closed round Hank's arm halting him in his stride. "Stay and help your ma."

Disappointment crossed Hank's face. "Aw, pa!" he protested.

"This is goin' to be no picnic for eighteen year olds," grinned a tall, well-built, rugged featured cowboy. "So, little brother, do as your pa says." He hurried after the men who streamed from the bunk-house and ran to get their horses.

Hank glared after his brother. "Bob always gets . . . " He stopped when he caught sight of his father's face, and saw him nod towards his mother. Hank knew better than to argue.

"You be all right, Meg?"

"Yes."

Al turned and strode towards the door. Meg watched him, words springing to her lips, but she did not speak, knowing that her husband wanted no words telling him to take care. She had known troubled days, had walked on the edge of fear of what might happen to her husband, but she had learned to live with these times, knowing that Al brooked no sympathy

20

on these occasions.

"Get some hot water, Hank." She sighed and turned back to the job of helping Jake until the doctor arrived.

She shuddered when she heard the thunder of hooves as Al led the Running W cowboys in fast ride for Sioux Hollow. She felt for the women who would suffer heartache when Al dealt with those responsible for Jake's beating.

They were grim-faced riders whose horses tore the earth in their gallop. Not a word was spoken. Each man was tense, knowing that a grim task had to be fulfilled.

As they neared the edge of Sioux Hollow, Al raised his hand and the cowboys pulled their horses to a halt at the top of the slope. The animals, panting after the hard run, snorted and pulled at the reins but the riders held them in check as they milled around.

Al took in the scene with one glance. It was exactly as Curly had described it, only the barbed wire had been fixed as far as the corner post and more stakes had been erected beyond the stream.

"Which one, Curly?" rapped Al.

"The tall, fair-haired one near the corner post."

Al nodded and eyed the man. The nesters, although they half expected this visit were nevertheless startled by the large number of riders and the suddenness of their appearance.

"Oh! No!" gasped Jamie.

"We've sure chosen a big one," muttered Will half to himself, a sickening feeling coming to his stomach.

Ben and Mart exchanged glances, fear of what form the reprisals might take showing in their eyes. Tom felt fear clutch his throat. He glanced round and saw Ben and Mart on the opposite side of the stream pick up their guns. "Fools!" he thought. "What chance have six against twenty?"

It was almost as if Mike had read his mind for he turned round and waved to Ben and Mart to put down their weapons. Mike turned back and stared at the line of riders. He knew it was useless to fight; it would only result in killings; better to back down and live to fight another day. Or should they move on again?

"Do we move on?" He put the question sharply to the three men beside him.

"We aren't going to have any peace here."

"If we want a home we'll have to."

"Can't do anything against that lot."

Mike said nothing. His jaw tightened. He had been determined that this would be the last time he would move but what good could he do if no one else was as determined? They had all said this would be the final place but now, when face to face with the test, they faltered. Who could blame them? Not he. Twenty riders on the hill were a mighty persuasive sight. All right, for their sakes he would move on, he would give in, better let the rancher know. Mike sighed and was about to step forward when the riders put their mounts down the hillside.

The pound of the horses drummed on the earth, getting louder and louder. The ground shook as the thunder got nearer and nearer. It vibrated into the very being, sending a chill searing through the body and a fear grasping at the mind. The show of strength had been seen on the hill-top and that would have been enough but there was something much more about this ride; this was no talking mission.

Jennie, standing with the other women beside the wagons, sensed it and fear gripped her heart. The sight of the twenty riders galloping down the hillside was bad enough but it was the thundering hooves which seemed to beat the fear into her. Suddenly she could stand it no longer. She broke from the group and started running towards her husband. Hands stretched out to restrain her, this was men's business, but she was gone, a forlorn figure on a landscape of tension.

As they neared the nesters four riders suddenly split from the group, swung round the corner post and rode faster down the hillside, splashed across the stream and ranged their horses round Ben Price and Mart Simpson, who twisted and turned to keep a close watch on the horsemen.

Al Barton pulled his powerful black to a halt in front of Mike Langton while the other riders spread out alongside him watching the nesters carefully. Only one man broke from the line. Bob Barton stabbed his horse forward, and with a huge grin on his face swung the animal across Jennie's path. Jennie pulled up sharply and twisted to get round the animal, but Bob pulled the horse round to stop her. She tried to turn again and again but each time Bob skilfully put the horse in her way. He laughed at the exasperation and annoyance on Jennie's face.

"That's goin' to be no place for ladies," he said smoothly and, before Jennie knew what was happening, Bob was out of the saddle and holding her tightly round the waist. "Better stay here with me." Jennie struggled but it was useless; she was restrained by a strong grip. "A little spitfire," whispered Bob in her ear. "I like "em that way."

As soon as he saw Bob Barton hindering his wife with his horse, Mike started to turn.

"Wouldn't if I were you," boomed Al, but Mike took no notice. He started towards his wife. His face grim, his first purpose of trying to avoid conflict gone. No man harassed his wife and got away with it.

Al signalled to one of his men. Quickly he unloosed his lariat and with skilful manipulation sent the lasso neatly over Langton. A quick pull and the rope tightened around him, pinning his arms to his side, before he realized what had happened. A sharp jerk and Mike was tumbled to the ground, kicking and squirming, trying to free himself of the rope as he was hauled through the grass until he was in front of Al. The nesters who had started to his aid found themselves halted by the threat of Colts.

As soon as the pull stopped, Mike scrambled to his feet.

"Stop that cowpoke from molesting my wife," he yelled, glaring at Al who sat heavy in the saddle, staring down at the dishevelled, dust-covered nester. "It ain't her quarrel."

"She'll not be harmed," said Al.

Mike turned to see if his wife was all right. His anger boiled when he saw Bob's arms round her.

"Let her go," he yelled at Bob, "or I'll . . ."

"You'll what?" sneered Bob. "You ain't in a position to do anything."

Mike's lips tightened grimly and he tried once again to free himself from the rope only to be reminded it was useless by a sudden pull, which jerked him off his feet.

"All right," shouted Al, "you men know what to do."

Six men left the line, started cutting the barbed wire and knocking down the posts, while four more rode quickly to the wagons. They dismounted and taking embers from the fire set fire to three of them. The women, seeing their belongings going up in smoke, looked anxiously at their menfolk who were helpless to do anything. As the cowboys rode back to join their fellow riders, sobs racked the bodies of the womenfolk.

Mike looked round desperately. He glared angrily at the man who sat immobile on his horse, finding himself hating this rancher who had swept in, backed by twenty men.

"I'll leave you one wagon so you can move on, nester. No man settles here."

"We've a right . . . " started Mike.

"You've no right," cut in Al harshly. "This is free range, range that I use and other ranchers use, it's not for farmers."

"Legally we've . . . "

28

"Don't come with your legal talk, that don't count around here. You're moving and moving soon but first you've got to be taught a lesson! You don't beat up one of my men and get away with it!" There was no disguising the menace and the threat in Al's voice.

It sent a chill into the men held at bay and Jennie's gasp of "Oh! No!" made Bob Barton chuckle with a reply of, "Oh! Yes!" whispered in her ear.

Al signalled to two men. They dismounted and ran to Mike, pinned his arms to his side and released the lasso. On Al's signal four other men climbed from their saddles and quickly laid out four long lengths of barbed wire with about a foot between the lengths. The two men holding Mike forced him, against his struggles, to one end of the barbed wire. Two other cowboys grabbed his feet and, in spite of Mike's resistance, he was lifted bodily and dropped unceremoniously across the barbed wire.

He recoiled instinctively as the barbs bit through his clothes and pierced his flesh. Mike tried to get up but a sharp kick in the ribs put an end to his attempt and, almost before he realized it, he was rolled over twice so that the barbed wire wrapped itself round him. Mike winced as more and more barbs bit into his flesh being driven in afresh with every movement as he was rolled the full length of the wire. His clothes were ripped and his flesh torn. Blood flowed and the pain screamed through his body with every turn. When they reached the end of the wire Mike was one entangled mass and for a few minutes more he was rolled back and forth.

As the men started on Mike, Jennie tried to struggle and Bob, enjoying the feel of her body allowed her the slightest encouragement. Tears flowed as she watched her husband's torture and the tension mounted in her until she could hold it no longer.

"Stop it! Stop it!" she screamed, but

the cowboys went on with their task as if she had not been there.

Will could stand it no longer. He started forward in spite of the menacing guns. A Colt roared and dust spurted at his feet pulling him up short.

"Move again and the bullet's for you," warned Al icily.

Will glared at the rancher who remained unmoved as he returned his attention to Mike.

"All right," he called. Jennie felt relief that it was all over and she stopped her struggles but she stiffened with horror as Al shouted his next command. "Take him to the top of the hill."

Jennie's eyes widened unbelievingly. "Oh! No!" she moaned.

Four cowboys picked Mike up, carefully avoiding the hated barbed wire. Silence, except for the crackling flames from the blazing wagons, spread across Sioux Hollow. The small group moved slowly up the hillside until they reached the top. They dropped

Mike on to the ground and with two sharp shoves sent him rolling down the hillside. Pain screamed through his body as each turn ripped his flesh. It bit deep, driving into his very nerves. His mind whirled faster and faster until he was lost in its blur and he knew no more.

Jennie stared in horror at the whirling mass of barbed wire as it hurled down the hillside, until it stopped a few feet away. The gasp choked in her mouth at the sight of the lacerated body of her husband. She retched and lost consciousness.

Al turned to Curly. "Which two held Jake?" he asked curtly.

Curly pointed out Tom and Will who were seized and lashed to two stakes. Their shirts were ripped from their backs and on Al's order of 'Five each', the whips cracked and lashed, tearing big gashes across the backs of the nesters. The women by the wagon moaned and turned their heads away, seeking comfort from each other, but they could not shut out the sound of the whips. Tom and Will jerked with every slash as the thongs drove pain searing into their bodies. With the final stroke they hung limp in their bonds.

Al ordered his men to mount their horses, then paused for a moment staring at young Jamie, whose ashen face showed the horror and revulsion he felt at the punishment inflicted on his friends. Al saw a youngster the same age as his own son but he felt no remorse that the boy had witnessed the happenings. This was a man's world and a boy had to become a man sometime.

"You any relation to these folks?" Al asked.

Jamie gulped, licked his lips, then spoke up. "My brother-in-law." He nodded in the direction of Mike.

"Then tell your brother-in-law to be away from here by morning, and the rest of them, we want no nesters here." He glanced in the direction of Bob who was supporting Jennie as she regained consciousness. "Go and help your sister, boy."

Jamie's hesitation was only momentary. It was a hesitation born of confusion at the happenings and the scene around him, where only a short while ago all had been peaceful. Then he turned and ran to Jennie.

"Take care of her, boy," grinned Bob. "If she wants to stay, I'll be back."

The words penetrated Jennie's dazed mind and she glared angrily at Bob as he turned to his horse. He swung into the saddle, looked down on the sister and brother, his handsome features broken by a broad grin. His blue eyes flashed and he laughed hard as he rode passed them to join the other cowboys who were already putting their animals up the slope.

"You all right, sis?" asked Jamie.

Jennie nodded. She drew a deep breath and looked around, only to recoil with horror at the sight of Tom and Will hanging limp against the stakes, their backs reddening with blood flowing from the deep lash marks.

"Oh! Jamie! What have we come to?" She grasped his hand and hurried to the barbed wire bundle which was her husband. Jennie and her brother fell on their knees beside him searching for some way to relieve the unconscious form but thankful that he was not aware of his suffering at this moment. Jennie fought back the desire to break down and cry. That would not help matters. She looked at her younger brother who was staring, horrified by the mangled mess of wire, flesh and blood caked with dust.

"Wire cutters, Jamie?" Jennie's voice was sharp, taking command of the situation, demanding her brother to be active to take his mind off Mike.

Jamie ran to find the necessary implement and Jennie glanced around Sioux Hollow.

Martha Byron and Bess King had reached their husbands, and, helped by Ben Price and Mart Simpson, were lowering them gently to the ground. Ethel Price was hurrying towards her, concern and pity showing on her face. Jennie saw Ben speak quickly to Mart and glance in her direction. They spoke to the two women who nodded and then the two men ran towards Jamie. Smoke curled from the ruins of the wagons, a desolate backcloth to the grim scene.

As quickly as they dare, Mike's friends clipped the wire and removed it carefully from his body. Jennie hoped Mike would remain unconscious until the awful, patience-demanding task was completed but they were only half-way through when Mike stirred. His face screwed with pain as his movement renewed the hurt and brought unconsciousness flooding back.

"Keep still, darling." The voice was soft, gentle and commanding.

Mike looked in its direction and Jennie came sharply into focus above his head and he realized that she was kneeling, cradling his head in her lap and holding him gently but firmly. Then he suddenly remembered what had happened. The horror of his experience hit him and he knew why his whole body felt so sore and why he still felt the pain of barbed wire in his back. He looked round, careful not to move and he saw Ben and Mart and then Jamie and Ethel. All were looking at him, concern and compassion on their faces.

"Hold still, Mike, we've nearly finished the front and then we'll do your back. All right?" said Ben.

Mike mustered a wan smile. "Yes."

"Get a blanket from the wagon, Jamie," said Mart. "We'll need it for Mike to lie on when we do his back."

A few minutes later the last piece of wire was removed from Mike's legs, and the blanket laid alongside him. Ben and Mart turned Mike over as gently as they could and laid him on his stomach. The movement hurt but Mike hid the pain.

"What the . . . ?" Mike gasped when

he saw the group of four people a short distance away. Tom and Will had regained consciousness and were sitting up, but their wives were still administering to their gashed backs.

"They whipped Will and Tom for helping in the beating you gave the cowboy," explained Jennie.

"Oh, no!" The words escaped from Mike's lips in one low whisper of regret.

Another hour passed before the torture of snipping wire clippers and the persuasive removal of embedded barbs was over. During that time Mike had suffered agonies but had also expressed his sorrow and regrets to Tom and Will who, when their wives could do no more had come over to see how Mike was.

"Ethel, some boiled water," requested her husband as their task was near completion. "Jamie, hitch the horses to the wagon; we'll have to take these three to the doctor."

As soon as Mike had been carefully

bathed by Jennie's gentle hands he was helped to his feet and into the wagon which Jamie had brought over, after gathering together their few remaining belongings.

Ben and Mart rounded up the rest of their horses and, with Jamie driving the wagon, the nesters set out for town.

The wagon rumbled for a hundred yards along the hollow and then took the rough track up the gentler part of the slope. The party was silent, each lost in their own thoughts. As the wagon reached the top of the rise Mike looked back on Sioux Hollow.

His eyes swept the grassland seeing it as he had done for the first time, seeing the home he had planned and the land he had fenced and a short distance away spread along the hollow those of Tom, Ben, Will and Mart all near enough to be neighbourly; a little settlement of farmers, each independent but each willing and eager to help the other as times demanded.

Now all he saw were broken fences

and the charred remains of three wagons. Where two days ago there had been dreams now there was disillusionment and a tortured body to remind him.

His lips tightened in a thin, grim line and his eyes narrowed.

"I'll not run," he muttered. "I'll not run."

3

THE main street of Wainwright was fairly busy as the nesters' wagon, followed by Ben and Mart with the horses, tumbled slowly through the dust of the dry, dirt roadway. The stagecoach had just arrived and about twenty people were gathered around it outside the stageline's office. A group of six women gossiped outside the store. When the wagon pulled up at the doctor's, the wounded men attracted considerable attention as they climbed out on to the roadway and stepped on to the sidewalk.

There were mutterings among the people wondering what had happened, but there were no murmurings of sympathy. This was a cow-town, founded and prospering on the cattle trade, dependent for its livelihood on the ranches in the vicinity. The nesters were recognized for what they were, and too many people earned good money because of the ranchers to sympathize with the newcomers. They were regarded as a threat and a menace by the majority who saw with a reduction in cattle-land a reduction in prosperity. Only a few saw that change must come and could bring improvement for all.

After a few brief words Mart accompanied the beaten men into the doctor's while the rest of the party remained outside as objects of curious glances from passers-by.

Dr White was horrified at the men's condition. "Who did this?" he demanded as he and his wife busied themselves administering to the nesters' needs.

Mart described the rancher.

"Al Barton!" said the doc. "You sure bucked the wrong guy there. What happened?"

Mart related the incidents, to which the doctor only grunted, now and then, as he went about his job quickly and efficiently.

When Mart had finished the doctor glanced at him. "Will you go and tell the sheriff I want to see him right away?

"Sure." Mart hurried from the house and, after a brief word of assurance to those waiting at the wagon, he crossed the street and sought out the sheriff's office.

The lawman glanced up from the papers he was studying when Mart entered his office.

"Sorry to interrupt, sheriff," said Mart, "but Doc White said would you come over to his house immediately."

The sheriff was a little surprised that the town's doctor should send a message with someone who was obviously a nester.

"Why?" he queried.

"Just said for me to fetch you," replied Mart.

The sheriff grunted and picked up his Stetson. He supposed it must be important for Doc White to send for him, but a nester — ? As he accompanied Mart to the doctor's the sheriff was aware of the glances of curiosity which came in his direction from folks along the street, but he made no comment and cast only a cursory glance at the nesters beside the wagon as he turned through the white gate into the doctor's garden.

A few minutes later the sheriff was confronting Doc White.

"What's it all about, doc?" he asked.

"Wanted you to see the way these men have been treated."

The sheriff's eyes widened with surprise when he saw the ugly gashes and lacerations.

"What happened? Who are you? Where you from?" He shot the questions sharply.

Mike spoke up introducing his companions and himself.

The sheriff nodded to each one. "Wal, to keep the record straight I'm Chris Lever. Now, your story."

Mike told it quickly and precisely and all the time he was trying to weigh up the man in front of him but all he came up with was his superficial appearance, a man of medium height, dark-brown hair, square faced with dull, brown eyes. There was nothing outstanding about him, nothing which impressed and yet to hold the job of sheriff he must have some ability, unless . . . But Mike dismissed that thought; only better knowledge of the man would fill that one.

The sheriff pursed his lips and rubbed his chin thoughtfully when Mike had finished. He had heard of nester troubles in other areas but, even though he knew they would come eventually to Wainwright, he had pushed the thoughts to the back of his mind. Now trouble was with him!

He glanced at Mike. "Guess you'll be movin' on after this." The words were half a question, half a hopeful statement. If the nesters went on their way he would be relieved of an awkward situation.

The doctor glanced at the sheriff but made no comment. Mike recognized the desire for no trouble in the lawman and, although he had not consulted his companions on the situation, he gave his answer.

"No. I figure we have a right and I intend to stay!"

The sheriff gasped. "But after what you've been through."

"If I've got a right no man's going to do me out of it, and this country's taken my fancy."

"Barton will fight; you've seen what he can do; you've seen his strength. You're no match for that, never will be," pointed out Lever.

"But we've right on our side," insisted Mike.

"What good is right against the likes of Barton?" emphasized the sheriff.

"You're the lawman, you tell me," replied Mike.

Doc White smiled. "He's got you there, Chris."

"Look here, Langton, I can go out to

the Running W, I can arrest Barton, but where does that get anybody? Barton could resist, he's got the force to do so, but he wouldn't, he'd play it cool. He has good standing around here and playing it that way would gain him a lot of sympathy, then comes a trial and no cattlemen jury, in a cattle town, in cattle country is going to convict a cattleman for teaching some nesters a lesson." Objections at this last remark sprang to Mike's lips but the lawman quietened him down with a wave of his hand. "Hold on. Yes, a lesson, after all you beat up one of his men and no cattleman is going to stand by and see that happen. If I arrest him I've got to arrest you and where does that put you? Is a cattleman jury going to let you off?"

"But this is all one sided," protested Mike.

"Sure it is," agreed the sheriff. "No one could deny it, but who's goin' to alter it? Ranchers are mighty powerful people around here. My advice to you is move on."

"Did you advise the family that's moved into Sundance Hollow to do the same?" asked the doctor.

"No. I've had no cause to, there's been no trouble there," replied Lever.

"So the nesters have a right; no trouble and that's all right by you, trouble and they're advised to move on," said Mike.

The sheriff nodded. "That just about sizes it up. I'm sorry, Langton, but that's the way of it."

Mike could sympathize with the sheriff's dilemma. Buck against the cattlemen, especially a powerful one like Al Barton, and he could be out of a job. Maybe he wasn't run by the cattlemen but if things blew against them they could make it mighty uncomfortable for him. No doubt he kept law and order but anything big, then the cattleman's views counted a lot.

"Well, isn't Sundance Hollow, your answer?" put in Doc White.

"You mean settle there?" asked Mike.

"Why not? There's land for all of you there. It's similar to Sioux Hollow."

"And what about the rancher who runs cattle on that land, isn't he going to kick?" asked Mike.

"I doubt it," put in Lever quickly, seeing a possible trouble-free answer if these nesters were determined to stay. "Zeke Hedley uses it but he's not objected so far, in fact I hear tell he's started to fence himself."

"Sundance Hollow it could be," mused Mike but he still realized it was open range and if Hedley was friendly Al Barton and other advocates of open range could cause trouble.

The sheriff left the doctor's satisfied that he had not been forced into a confrontation with Al Barton, but he was somewhat worried that the nester problem would blow up again some time in the future. The nesters were moving west and sooner or later a collision would come, but Chris Lever hoped the problem would have sorted itself out before then. It could have come through Mike Langton and his party but now that might have been averted, Zeke Hedley seemed to have a more tolerant outlook.

Half an hour later Doctor White was satisfied that he had done all he could.

"You'll all have to take it easy for a few days," he said as he handed them a box of salve. "Put this on each day, but if anything shows signs of not healing come back to me.

The men were appreciative of the doctor's help.

"Where do you stand in this cattle country, doc?" asked Mart.

Doc White eyed him shrewdly. "Men and women are all human beings to me no matter what their following."

"A pity there aren't more around like you," put in Will. "This is the fourth move we've made, pushed on by cattlemen."

"They've been a law unto themselves

for so long they don't want a change. Understandable, though, and maybe we'd all be the same if we saw our way of life threatened. There are only a few folks around here who are not biased in their views, they see that change is inevitable. Zeke Hedley is one of them, though what his opinions might be if nesters crowd him too much or if other ranchers get rough I can't say."

"If he's fencin' his land," put in Tom, "seems to me he's prepared to cut down on the land he can use and tolerate nesters on the other."

"Sure," agreed the doc, "but don't forget that you'd still be moving on to open range, still be fencing what a cattleman claims is his right; you could still have bother from other ranchers even if you are much farther away from the area they usually ride."

"You mean Al Barton might still try to push us?" said Mike.

Doc White nodded. "Might just do that, especially when you've already tangled with him."

51

Mike grunted. "Anywhere in town we can get fixed up with wagons?"

"Wes Tyburn along at the end of the street. Store's half-way between here and Tyburn's if you want outfitting."

"Thanks," said Mike. "We'll see if we can get fixed up."

The four men left the doctor's to rejoin those who were anxiously waiting outside. They quickly reassured their wives that they were all right and then put everyone in the picture regarding the possibility of settling in Sundance Hollow.

"But surely we aren't staying around here after what has happened." It was Martha Byron who voiced the words.

"Where do we go?" said Mike. "We've got to stop running sometime. We all agreed Sioux Hollow was the place when we saw it."

"But we didn't expect beatings and whippings," pointed out Martha.

"No, we didn't," agreed Mike, "but I think we shall stay in spite of that."

"Do you think we'll ever be able to

settle down free and easy?" exclaimed Bess King. "Haven't we been fools ever to think of coming west?" The words choked in her throat and she bit her lip hard as her eyes filled with tears.

Will put a comforting arm round his wife. "Steady on, Bess. We knew life wouldn't be easy. Is anything worth having if it isn't worth fighting for?" He looked at Mike. "I take it you're staying; if so, I'll stay."

"I was thinking that way," answered Mike, "but it will depend on Jennie and Jamie." He glanced at his wife and brother-in-law.

Jennie bit her lip. She had been dreading this moment of decision. She had sensed all along that Mike didn't want to run like a whipped dog, and yet all her instinct cried out to leave, to get as far away from this place as possible. "What happened once could happen again," she spoke in a low voice half to herself.

"It could," agreed Mike, "but . . . "

"I know what you are going to say,

Mike, but I fear the future, I fear what might happen to you or to Jamie, but that might happen anywhere we go." She looked hard at her husband. "If you want to stay, I'll stay with you."

There was a deep expression of love and gratitude as Mike said, "Thank you, Jennie." He turned to Jamie. "What about you?"

"I'll stay," the youngster replied.

Mike smiled and slapped him on the shoulder. "Good lad."

"I'm with you," spoke up Tom Byron who received a smile of encouragement from his wife.

"How about you, Ben?" asked Mike, his glance embracing Ben's wife as well.

Ben and Ethel glanced at each other before Ben spoke. "We're tired of moving; we want to settle down. I think Ethel's brother feels the same."

"Sure do," confirmed Mart to make it a unanimous decision to stay.

"Good," smiled Mike, pleased that the little group, which had journeyed west in search of new homes, would stick together and be neighbours. "I figure we'd better replace our wagons."

The men agreed and soon the wagon was pulling up outside the last building in Wainwright.

Wes Tyburn eyed the nesters as they approached him and to their query he put the question bluntly. "Got the money?"

Mike nodded. "We aren't penniless nesters if that's what you're thinking. We came west with plenty to set us up."

"Then the wagons are yours."

The deal completed, the horses were soon hitched to the wagons and the procession trundled back down the street to the store. After obtaining their supplies they headed out of Wainwright in the direction of Sundance Hollow, watched by a number of townsfolk and cowboys who wondered.

When they reached Sundance Hollow, Mike halted the wagons so that they could survey the land. They saw a long shallow depression running east and west and Mike guessed that it got its name from the fact that the rays of the rising and setting sun would seem to dance along the hollow as it rose above and dropped below the horizon. A small stream ran westwards with the deepening of the hollow. Although Mike preferred the deeper Sioux Hollow with more protection from its higher sides and with its wider stream, he figured this was not a bad place and the land looked good. It was a much longer hollow than the one they had been forced to leave and they saw no sign of the family mentioned by the doctor.

"I figure anywhere should suit us," called Tom. "Let's get down to the stream."

The wagons creaked and squeaked their way down the slope and before long they were placed beside the stream and their occupants were making camp.

When Ben was satisfied that everything was in order he left his wagon and

56

sought out Mike. "Mart and I figured it might be a good idea to see this here Zeke Hedley; we might avert a bit of trouble and maybe establish a friendly relationship," he suggested.

"A good idea, Ben," agreed Mike, "I'll come along, reckon I'll manage the ride."

They told the others of their proposal and they soon had three horses saddled.

"Be careful, Mike," said Jennie as Mike bade her goodbye.

He smiled reassuringly, swung into the saddle and the three men put their horses at a steady trot along the hollow.

After two miles they encountered barbed wire and turned their horses to the corner post half-way up the hillside. They followed the wire along the hillside and, after a farther mile, spotted a wagon beside the stream. Finding a gate they let themselves through and rode towards the wagon. As they approached a man appeared from the far side of the wagon and was followed a moment later by a woman and two boys. He eyed the riders suspiciously as they got nearer and Mike noted his hand did not stray far from the butt of his Colt.

"Howdy," greeted Mike with a smile as he pulled his horse to a halt. "Thought we'd make ourselves known when we saw your wagon. I'm Mike Langton, this here's Ben Price and his brother-in-law Mart Simpson. We figure on settling farther along the hollow. There are another two families. We've just pulled in. Thought we'd ride over and make the acquaintance of Zeke Hedley."

The man stepped forward and Mike could sense the tension go out of the group. He held out his hand which Mike leaned down and took in a firm grip.

"Pete Nicholson," he said. "This is my wife Myra and Billy, twelve, and Dan, eleven."

Mike and Ben nodded their greetings with a smile.

"Have a cup of coffee?" asked Myra pleasantly.

"Well, that's mighty nice of you, Mrs Nicholson," said Mike. "We don't want you to go to any trouble."

"It's no trouble. I just made some."

"Right then. Thank you very much."

The three men climbed from their horses and were soon exchanging views and enjoying the coffee.

"Had any trouble since you arrived?" asked Mike.

"No," replied Pete, "but I must say things aren't too friendly for homesteaders around here. We've felt a hostility whenever we've been in town but never had any difficulty in getting what we want."

"We tried Sioux Hollow but got rough treatment from a rancher by the name of Al Barton," said Ben, without going into details, which he figured would alarm Mrs Nicholson and her sons.

Pete nodded. "I've heard of him but he hasn't been around here, maybe figures we're too far from his spread and that we're more of a problem to Zeke Hedley."

"What's his attitude?" queried Mike.

"Well you couldn't say he was outright friendly nor could you figure him to be hostile." Pete paused thoughtfully. "I put it tolerant but maybe he sees farther ahead than most others around here, maybe he reckons the nester is here to stay and nothing the rancher does will stop him; eventually rancher and nester are going to have to live side by side."

"Aye, you're right there but there could be a heap of trouble before that happens," commented Ben.

"Hedley must be providing for that future — he's fencing."

"That could make him unpopular with other ranchers," observed Mart.

"Could do." Pete paused and looked hard at the newcomers before he went on. "But I don't know what his attitude will be with more nesters coming into Sundance Hollow. Don't get me wrong," Pete added hastily, "I'm not trying to get you to move on."

Mike looked thoughtful. "Well we'll see what Hedley has to say. Tell you what. If he isn't too favourable, we'll move on, we don't want trouble for you, but we did have our minds set on around here. We're tired of moving on."

"Then stick it out," said Pete. "Don't leave on our account. It will be nice to have some neighbours."

After Pete gave them directions Mike, Ben and Mart bade the Nicholsons goodbye and, before long, were riding past the sign which announced they had reached the Circle C ranch. A few moments later they were pulling to a halt outside the long, low ranch-house under the studying gaze of several cowboys.

They were about to dismount when a man in his fifties stepped out of the house. His hair and moustache were greying and his rugged, weather-beaten face spoke of a life in the open. He still cut a good figure with little surplus fat on him.

"Howdy," he greeted.

Leather creaked as Mike and Ben swung out of the saddle.

"Mike Langton, Ben Price and Mart Simpson, Mr Hedley." Mike introduced as he mounted the steps and felt his hand taken in a firm grip. He felt the penetrating look of the dark-brown eyes and knew he was dealing with a shrewd, no nonsense man but one from whom he felt he would get a fair deal.

"You've taken the trouble to find my name before you've come here. Nesters, aren't you?"

There was neither friendliness nor hostility in his voice as he used that word.

"Yes," replied Mike. "We've pulled into Sundance Hollow, figured we might settle there but thought we'd ride over here, make your acquaintance and see how the land lies."

"See whether I'm hostile or not,

say what you mean, son, say what you mean. You didn't want the same treatment as Al Barton gave you."

"Seems you've done some checking up too," returned Mike.

Zeke smiled. "No, but some of my men heard about it in town, an' you fit the description." He paused, eyeing Mike carefully. "Well, now, that's free range in Sundance Hollow so you can please yourself and, provided you don't buck me, I'll not worry you, but I can't say for other ranchers around here."

"That's great, Mr Hedley," said Mike enthusiastically with a grin at Ben.

"Now don't go thinkin' everything's lovely. As I say that's open range so any rancher around here can use it. Mind you there's always been a bit of an understanding, I've used most of Sundance Hollow an' Al Barton's used Sioux Hollow."

"So he can't beef about it if we settle in Sundance," put in Ben.

"Wal, that ain't necessarily so," replied Zeke.

"So if he cuts up rough it's 'cos he hates nesters," said Mart. "He really doesn't need to use it."

"Wal, you said it, not me," said Zeke with a smile.

"What about you and Sundance?" asked Ben.

"Wal, let me put it this way. I reckoned if nesters could fence off land so could I and I'd do it before too many nesters got here and I was left with no ranch. I'm in the process of fencing off sufficient to keep the Circle C a going concern and Sundance Hollow has not come into my reckonin'."

Mike smiled. "Thanks, Mr Hedley. We're mighty grateful to you for being so straight with us. We know exactly where we stand. I hope all will be well between us."

"So do I," replied Zeke. "But don't forget I'm very much a cattleman at heart, and I can sympathize with my fellow ranchers, though I think they're fools for not looking farther than their nose-ends and doin' what I'm doin', fencin' to a size which suits their needs."

The three nesters were bidding Zeke goodbye when the door of the house opened and a dark-haired, young woman came out.

"Sorry, Dad, I didn't know you had someone with you. I was just coming to tell you everything is ready."

"Thanks, Joan. You'd better meet Mike Langton, Ben Price and Mart Simpson they're going to try farming in Sundance."

Joan smiled her welcome, her eyes hesitating a moment when they met Mart's. She judged him to be about her own age and good looking. Mart saw a pretty girl with an open, friendly face, simply but attractively dressed in a patterned gingham frock.

"We're just going, miss," said Mike after they had exchanged greetings, "so we'll not hold your father up."

They turned and went down the steps and had reached their horses when the sound of hooves attracted their attention. They glanced round to see two riders approaching at a steady trot. Mike stiffened as he recognized Al Barton and his son Bob. Ben glanced anxiously at Mike, and Zeke was not slow in recognizing the tension which had come into the three nesters.

They waited and watched. The two horsemen pulled to a halt in front of the verandah. Al nodded to Zeke but his face betrayed his fury at the sight of Mike.

"Thought I told you to clear out of here," rasped Al, glaring down at Mike, "or didn't that kid brother-in-law of yours give you my message?"

"He did." Mike met Barton's gaze. "You said by morning, and we're out of Sioux Hollow."

"Then you've misunderstood me." Al paused, his eyes smouldering angrily. "I meant out of these parts," he boomed. "Do you understand that?"

Mike made no comment but turned to his horse and prepared to mount. Suddenly he felt a vicious push in his back and he was pressed hard against his own mount which whinneyed and stepped away.

With the pressure off Mike swung round, his eyes blazing furiously, to see Bob Barton looking down on him.

"Don't turn your back on my pa when he's talking to you," snapped Bob. "Do you want another lesson, nester?"

Mike stepped forward quickly and because retaliation was not expected Bob was taken completely unawares when Mike grabbed his arm and pulled viciously, to bring him tumbling from the saddle. He had no sooner hit the dust than Mike was grabbing him.

"Leave it, Barton!" As soon as Mart Simpson had seen Mike's movement his Colt flashed from its holster, and, even as Al's huge hand closed round the butt of his gun he found himself staring into the muzzle of a menacing gun.

As Mike dragged Bob off the ground he drove his fist hard into Bob's face.

The cowboy sprawled in the dust his eyes registering shocked surprise which turned to angry hate. He twisted on the ground his right hand snaking towards his gun, but even as it cleared leather Mike was upon him kicking viciously at the gun hand. The Colt was sent spinning from Bob's grasp and he rolled over grasping his hand trying to relieve the pain.

Mike stood over him, his chest heaving as he breathed heavily, his lips tightening in a thin line and a wildness touching his eyes. He was about to grab Bob again but stopped himself.

"Don't push me around again, Barton!" The words were harsh, carrying a threat. "And don't try to finger my wife again!"

Mike swung on his heel, walked to his horse and climbed into the saddle. "Come on, Mart, put that gun away; Barton won't draw now."

Mart hesitated a moment, slipped his Colt back into its holster and mounted his horse.

Mike looked hard at Al Barton who had remained silent but whose eyes reflected all the hate he knew for nesters.

"Don't push us any more," rapped Mike. "Sioux Hollow's burned into my mind and body!"

4

FOR a moment Al Barton watched the dust spurting from the hooves as the nesters galloped away. Then he turned to Zeke Hedley.

"What's them lousy coyotes doin' here?" he demanded.

Zeke ignored the authoritative note. "Stop sitting there like God Almighty an' come inside, Al," he said and turned towards the house. He smiled and winked at Joan as he did so. Then he stopped and glanced back at Bob who was still sitting on the ground fingering his mouth, tender and bleeding from the blows. "You come in too when you get up Bob. Joan'll fix that blood." He strolled into the house followed by his daughter.

Al glared at him, but realizing he was on the losing side, and that if he wanted to see Zeke Hedley, he had to do as Zeke had indicated. The leather groaned as his heavy weight swung out of the saddle.

Bob, fury welling at his defeat in front of Zeke and the Circle C cowboys and especially in front of Joan, pushed himself to his feet and beat the dust from his clothes. He picked up his gun and slammed it into his holster, before recovering his Stetson which he slapped hard against his leg as he walked to the house.

"Wal," thundered Al as he walked into the pleasantly furnished room where Zeke was waiting for him, a glass of whisky in his hand, "what were those nesters doin' here?"

"Here take this," said Zeke offering the whisky, "and sit down. There's one for you there Bob when Joan's fixed those cuts."

Bob muttered his thanks and followed Joan while his father lowered his bulky frame into a chair.

"Wal?" he asked again, but a little of the demand had gone from his voice, although Zeke could tell he was still annoyed at having another run in with Mike Langton and one in which he hadn't had the upper hand.

"They're thinking about settling in Sundance Hollow, rode in here to see what the situation was."

"You told them to ride on, I hope," said Al. "That's open range."

"I told them it was, but as far as I am concerned they could please themselves. Said I was the one that used it but wouldn't be doing so any more, but this didn't mean anybody else would be agreeable."

Al's eyes narrowed as he stared at Zeke. "You're encouraging them, Zeke!"

"They have a right . . ." started the owner of the Circle C.

"Rights be damned," burst out Al. "We've been here all these years usin' this land now these nesters move in, fence, and it's theirs. What about us? Have we just to sit by an' watch it

72

happen an' lose land we've used for years."

"Fence like I'm doin'," suggested Zeke.

There was a moment of tense silence then Al exploded. "So it's right. The rumour I heard that you were startin' to fence is right." His lips tightened as he stared angrily at Zeke. "You've no sense, you're playin' right into the nesters' hands. You're goin' against your own kind."

"I've plenty of sense if you would only see it. Nesters are bound to come and stay. You . . . "

"They certainly will with your encouragement," broke in Al.

"You may drive this lot off," continued Zeke, ignoring Al's interruption, "but there'll be more, big parties of nesters will come an' there could be hostilities. There'll be more land wanted and it will disappear under the plough if you don't fence off what you want now."

"Ranchers an' farmers will never get on side by side. This is good cattle country; we've always been used to open range and open range it's got to stay."

"Al, we've never needed all that range. I've worked out what I reckon I need an' that I'm fencin'."

"Maybe there's been more open range than we've needed in the past but what if anybody wants to expand. I'm certainly goin' to increase the size of my herd to offset bad times. If everybody around Wainwright decides likewise we'll need all the open range we can get an' fencin' isn't goin' to help matters." The door opened and Bob walked in. "Hi, Bob, it's right, Zeke has started to fence," Al informed his son.

"What!" Bob glared at Zeke. "You're no better than them goddamned nesters."

Zeke's eyes smouldered angrily. He wouldn't take that talk from a man of his own age let alone a whippersnapper like Bob, young enough to be his son.

"Careful what you say, Bob," he snapped hastily. "You might find yourself on the wrong end of the stick again."

The reference to his recent humiliation taunted Bob. He stiffened, his fist clenched and his eyes narrowed as he stared at Zeke.

"You know darned well that barbed wire is no good for cattle. If any of our steers are ripped by your wire you'll pay for it," he snarled.

"Not only that," put in Al. "You're encouraging nesters. If one comes there'll be more. They'll flood us out."

"Dad's right," Bob went on. "If you'd pushed the Nicholsons as soon as they arrived Langton and his crowd wouldn't be here now. I guess they heard in town that the Nicholsons hadn't been dealt with so figured they could use Sundance Hollow as well. After our treatment of Langton he'd have kept goin' if he hadn't had encouragement to stop."

"You didn't kick up a fuss when the Nicholsons arrived," pointed out Zeke.

"Wal, they were only one family, they were far enough away from us, but I see now it was a mistake. Letting them settle has opened the way for Langton and his crowd. Others will come. If they're made to see they're not wanted, that this is cattlemen's country, maybe we'll save the situation." He paused and looked hard at Zeke. "They're on land close to you, Zeke, land that you've used more than any of us so I figure it's up to you to push them."

"Now look here, Al, I . . . "

"No," cut in Bob roughly, "you look here. We pushed them off land we've used — Sioux Hollow, now I reckon all we ranchers should stick together an' keep them damned nesters movin'."

"Bob's right," said Al, pushing himself to his feet. "Get 'em out of Sundance, then there'll be no need for your wire."

Zeke said nothing. He knew it would be useless to argue further. Owning the biggest ranch in these parts, Al had always assumed an importance and an

76

authority that wasn't there, but other ranchers knew him and let the whole situation ride. There had never been any real reason for conflict but Zeke could see trouble ahead.

He walked to the verandah with the two men and silently watched them mount their horses.

"We'll be expectin' results," said Al. "An' before too long."

"Thank Joan fer patchin' me up," called Bob steadying his horse. "An' if you want help with Langton let me know; I'd like another go at him."

Father and son kicked their horses into a dust-stirring gallop away from the Circle C. Zeke's face was serious as he watched them go and didn't realize that Joan had come on to the verandah until he felt her arm slip through his.

"Things didn't go smooth then?" asked Joan seeing the look on her father's face.

"'Fraid not," replied Zeke. "Want me to move the nesters."

"But they've a right."

"I know," said Zeke. There was a certain sadness in his eyes. "If only the ranchers would fence, trouble could be avoided but they want open range. I can sympathize with them, I can see their point of view. It's a way of life and they don't want to change."

"What are you going to do, Dad?"

Zeke shook his head, "I don't know. I don't know." He paused looking thoughtful for a moment and then turned to Joan. "I know Bob Barton has been a bit sweet on you, you've grown up together, you see something of him from time to time, do you think it's likely to develop into anything more serious?"

Joan was a little taken aback by the question which came suddenly and, as far as she could see, had no connection with the subject they were talking about.

"Why Dad? What has this to do with it?"

"Well if — no you'd better answer my question before I say any more."

"Well, I don't know. Bob and I have known each other since we were kids, I suppose in cases like this love just grows without you realizing it, it doesn't just suddenly hit you." Joan paused, pursing her lips thoughtfully. "No, I'm not in love with Bob, I like him, I know he's got his bad side, he's bumptious, big-headed, thinks he knows it all but I reckon he'll mellow with age, but I don't think I'd ever want to marry him. He's friendly enough towards me, asked me to go to the dance with him next week as a matter of fact."

Zeke smiled at his daughter. She had a lot of common-sense; there was a wise head on those young shoulders. "Thanks for being forthright about it, Joan. I must say in one way I'm relieved. I don't think I'd like to see you married to Bob, he's getting too big for his boots and I'm not at all sure he'll mellow all that much."

"But what has all this to do with the nesters, Dad?" asked Joan.

"Wal if you were serious with Bob

then I just might move those nesters on; after all, a marriage with Bob would eventually mean a union of the two ranches, it so wouldn't do for me to go on with the fencin', that would lead to a heap of trouble even if I see it as the best way for the future."

"And now?" pressed Joan.

"The nesters have a right and so long as they don't cross me they can stay in Sundance Hollow as far as I'm concerned. If Barton wants to move them on it's up to him."

"But he won't want to use Sundance Hollow," Joan pointed out.

"I agree, but it is open range and Al will use that as an excuse. He's obsessed with the idea that if some nesters stay they'll all come flocking in. He forgets the land will take only so many and if he fences he could be all right."

"If only you could make them see, Dad."

Zeke shook his head rather sadly. "I've tried, but open range is a way of life from which it's hard to break, I know, it took me a lot of thinking before I decided to fence.".

"And courage," added Joan.

Zeke smiled. "Maybe we'll all need a lot of that before this job's over. Al wants me to move the nesters. If I don't there'll be trouble."

"For us?"

"I don't know. Maybe not. Maybe just for the nesters. Al Barton may not hit his own kind." Zeke hoped he sounded reassuring for Joan's peace of mind, but if he knew Al Barton correctly he figured Al's obsession of open range would blind him to everyone and everything else.

★ ★ ★

"A pity you tangled with Langton back there," said Al as he and his son headed for their ranch.

"I thought it might show him we mean business."

"But it backfired, didn't it," snapped

Al sarcastically. "Another time make sure you'll come out on top."

"Give me another chance an' I'll show that coyote, Langton."

"You might not get another chance if Zeke comes through."

"Do you think he'll push the nesters?"

Al rubbed his shin thoughtfully. "I'm not sure. He's a cattleman at heart but I don't like him fencin'."

"Maybe we should persuade him a little, eh pa?" grinned Bob.

"If it comes to it we just might. We'll give him a week to move them nesters on, then we'll think again."

They tapped their horses into faster speed and earth flew beneath the pounding hooves as they rode towards the Running W.

★ ★ ★

A week passed and the nesters were still in Sundance Hollow. They were beginning to feel more at ease, and as each day passed they relaxed a little more. Maybe their days of being pushed around were over. Maybe Al Barton had seen they were determined to stay and that, after Mike's handling of Bob, they would be no easy matter to move on.

The fencing of their land progressed steadily and as they became more and more certain that the cattlemen were not going to move them they started to discuss the houses they would build.

The Nicholsons were pleased to have some neighbours of their own kind and were delighted that the cattlemen had not moved in on them. It seemed that things were settling down and that the ranchers were prepared to let Sundance Hollow go.

"I figure I'll take me off to the dance in town tonight," announced Mart Simpson as the nesters were enjoying their evening meal.

"Do you think that's wise?" asked his sister.

"Why not?"

"There'll be a lot of cattlemen there,

they could cause trouble."

"I'll not be looking for it," pointed out Mart. "If there was going to be trouble the cattlemen would have pushed us by now. We can't remain isolated out here, we've got to move into the life around Wainwright and this is a good time to start."

"He's probably hoping that Joan Hedley will be there, been talking a lot about her since we were at the Circle C," said Ben with a grin.

"Now don't you go tangling with cattlemen over a girl," warned Mart's sister.

"I'll be all right, sis. It'll be good for nester-cattlemen relations."

When Mart rode into Wainwright later that evening it was already dark and lights were streaming from various buildings. He rode past the hall, from which the strains of the three-man band came as they played for the dancers, until he came to the saloon. There was plenty of noise coming from the room as he pushed through the batwings.

The saloon was full of cowboys and saloon-girls, tables were all occupied and the bar was lined almost full-length by cowboys who leaned on the long mahogany counter enjoying their drinks. Mart found a place near the corner and called for a beer. He was served quickly and civilly and, although he noticed one or two glances and nods in his direction, no one was antagonistic but neither were they friendly. He was just left alone. Mart took his time over the beer observing the life around him and then he left the saloon for the dance.

The hall was fairly full and Mart guessed it would really get crowded later on. He stood just inside the door for a while watching the dancing and again he knew that several remarks were made about him by various groups around the room.

He searched the dancers, who were enjoying a square dance, for Joan Hedley and then he saw her about half-way along the room. He was still watching her, admiring her slim figure and smiling face when the dance finished and an excuse me was announced. Mart saw Joan whirled into the waltz by Bob Barton. He edged his way forward to the dancing area and when the couple came round for the second time he stepped forward and halted them with a polite "Excuse me."

The two dancers stopped, Bob showing his amazement at the request. Joan sensed his annoyance and, realizing it could easily erupt in anger at the audacity of a nester to cut in on a cattleman, quickly took command of the situation. She left go of Bob's hand, at the same time thanking him with a disarming smile. She turned to Mart held out her hand which he took and as he put his right hand on her waist they moved into the waltz.

As they twirled Joan glanced back at Bob, smiling broadly at him and gave a slight shake of her head. Although he was seething angrily inside, he knew that Joan did not want him to create a scene so he respected her wishes.

For a few moments there was silence between the two dancers. Mart felt a little awkward and Joan felt rather pleased that this nester had requested a dance. She remembered seeing him at the ranch but even though he had made an impression then, he now seemed a little different. She figured it was seeing him dressed for the dance and the fact that his bright red shirt enhanced the bronzed, handsome face.

"I hope you didn't mind me cutting in?" said Mart making the question half an apology.

"Not at all," smiled Joan. "It is an excuse me."

"Your partner didn't like it," grinned Mart.

Joan laughed. "What could you expect after what happened at the Circle C."

"I suppose not," said Mart. "You remember me then."

"Of course; and I'd better warn

you Bob's still smarting after that humiliation at the hands of your friend."

"Mike Langton," prompted Mart.

"It's a good thing you were with him that day. You were quick on the draw. Where did you learn to handle a gun?"

"Back home. Ever since I was eighteen I reckoned I'd move west one day and I figured it might be useful to be able to draw first and shoot straight. Not that I believe in violence but I reckon a man has a right to defend what's his."

Joan nodded her head with a smile, approving of her partner's attitude. "Where are you from?" she asked.

"Little place called Eston way back east. My folks were farmers. I'd always had a hankering for a move so when they both died within a few weeks of each other and my sister and her husband were coming west I decided to come with them. We joined a small party Mike was forming from our neighbourhood and here we are."

"Getting settled in Sundance Hollow?"

"Yes. You must ride over and see us. I'd like you to meet my sister."

"Thanks. I will."

The music stopped, the dancers applauded and Bob Barton looked for Joan to return to him. Instead he saw Mart say something to her to which she replied with a nod. When Bob saw them walk over to the refreshment table his anger swelled, his fist clenched tightly and his lips drew into a hard thin line which bore ill-will for Mart Simpson.

Mart managed several dances with Joan during the rest of the evening and she was rather surprised that Bob made no more than a brief sarcastic observation on the fact. She had expected him to be more critical of her but maybe he realized that a scene at the dance would throw him up in a bad light.

Mart for his part was delighted with the way the evening went. He enjoyed every moment he spent with Joan and while no one was outright friendly towards him, several townsfolk did have a few words with him and no one was offensive. Mart reckoned it had been a good evening in establishing a better relationship between the nesters and the people amongst whom they had come to settle. Mart would have liked to have offered to escort Joan back to the Circle C but he knew this would only precipitate trouble with Bob Barton, for Bob had brought Joan to the dance and would no doubt be taking her home.

So Mart bade her goodnight, reminding her of her promise to visit their little gathering in Sundance Hollow, and left the hall as the last dance started.

He felt pleased with himself as he strolled slowly along the sidewalk towards his horse which he had left outside the saloon. He was listening to the sound of the music wishing that he was still dancing with Joan.

So occupied, he was taken completely

by surprise when, as he was passing the alley by the side of the blacksmith's shop, two men grabbed him and pulled him into the shadows.

He found himself held in a vice-like grip by two men who had their neckerchiefs pulled around the lower half of their faces. They forced him quickly along the alley to the back of the blacksmith's shop where Mart noticed that the door had been forced open. He was pushed roughly inside, staggered and fell to the floor. Anger seethed inside him as he got to his feet, his fists clenched tightly ready to do battle. As he straightened, he stiffened. He hadn't only two men to contend with for another three men, similarly disguised, stood in front of him. He was in for a beating but he would give a good account of himself before he finally succumbed to their attentions. He would get the first blow in. But, even as he was about to launch himself at the nearest man, he felt his arms grabbed again.

"Bring him over here," a voice, partially muffled by a neckerchief, ordered.

Mart was forced forward close to the forge's fire. His eyes widened with horror and he recoiled with the shock when he saw the cauldron of tar on the fire and, standing on the floor close to it, a bucket of feathers!

He struggled but it was useless. He was held too tightly.

"Don't like the look of that?" laughed one of the men.

"Wal, it'll teach you to keep away from the boss's daughter."

Mart was shaken. Circle C men! He had never expected this.

"That's her choice," he spat angrily.

A hand slashed sharply across his mouth.

"Don't you even dare talk of her. Your lips ain't fit to speak her name." The voice was vicious. "And remember, Circle C don't want to see you around here again."

The two men holding his arms forced

him to the floor and there, as he was unable to do anything, his legs were grabbed by two of the others, and tied tightly. A cloth was tied round his mouth and after his hands were fastened behind his back he was tied to an upright post by the fire.

One of the men picked up a long brush and dipped it into the tar.

* * *

Ethel Price stirred. She was only half asleep. Her brother was later than she expected and the worry had kept full sleep at bay. A few minutes passed and then relief flooded her tensed body when she heard the hoof beats, but almost immediately she stiffened again. There was more than one horse and they were riding fast. She slipped from between the blankets and pushed the canvas covering apart at the end of the wagon. She saw the riders silhouetted against the sky at the top of the slope and then they were lost against the hillside but their hoof beats thundered louder.

Alarm gripped her. "Ben, Ben," she cried as she stepped quickly to the still sleeping form of her husband. She shook him. "Ben, Ben, wake up." The man stirred and then the urgency in his wife's voice pierced his dulled mind, and he was awake, alert and hearing the pound of hooves.

"What is it?" he called as he got to his feet quickly. He grabbed for his rifle.

The hoof beats slowed. Ben pulled aside the canvas flap and with his rifle held ready looked out. The riders were close enough to be distinguishable. All except one were pulling their horses round. In a moment it was all over. The riders had turned and were galloping away as fast as they had approached, leaving the lone horse still coming towards the wagons.

Ben waited a moment and then he saw the rider was slumped across his horse. Alarm seized him.

"Stay there, Ethel!" he yelled and jumped from the wagon. He raced towards the horse. Reaching the animal he grabbed at the bridle calling to it to stop. A quick glance told Ben that the slumped form was Mart.

"Tarred and feathered!" The words hissed from Ben's lips in a gasp of horror at the sight of his brother-in-law.

He was only aware of the men from the other wagons when they reached his side. Their gasps spoke of the revulsion they felt at the treatment Mart had received.

"See who they were?" someone asked.

"No. There were five of them."

The hoof beats fading into the night mocked the nesters as they sought for identification.

Ethel pushed her way roughly through the little knot of men beside the horse. "Oh, no! no!" she gasped, the sobs racking her body.

"Steady, Ethel, steady." Ben grasped

his wife in his strong arms.

"Is he . . . is he . . . ?" She could not bring herself to speak the word she dreaded.

"I don't know," replied Ben.

Eager, helping hands were already lifting Mart from the horse and lowering the tarred and feathered figure to the ground. The other women were quickly on the scene anxious to help in any way they could. Mike bent over the silent form and, after a moment of time which seemed like eternity to the others, announced, "He's alive."

Ethel gasped and tears of relief flowed from her eyes.

"I don't think we can handle him, we'd better get him to the doc," said Mike as he straightened. "Ben and I will take him in."

"I must come too," Ethel's voice was sharp and anxious.

"It might be better if you stayed," said Mike gently.

"No. I must be there, if anything happens I — "

"All right, Ethel. I understand." Mike glanced at Ben who nodded.

"I'll get the wagon," said Ben.

Tom, Will and Jamie hurried away with Ben and they soon had the horses hitched to the wagon.

Once Mart had been lifted gently inside the wagon Mike lost no time in getting to town, using the greatest speed he dare.

Wainwright was in darkness when they arrived and it was a few minutes before their anxious knocking roused the doctor.

Doc White was still half asleep and annoyed at being woken in the middle of the night but, as soon as the nesters told him what had happened, he was alert, full of attention and sympathy.

Mike and Ben carried Mart inside the house and after a brief examination the doctor began the slow and laborious task of removing the tar and the feathers. He watched the unconscious Mart anxiously as he worked but, apart from one brief moment, which occurred after Mart momentarily regained consciousness, all was well.

It was over two hours later that the doctor was satisfied and started to swathe Mart in bandages. When he had finished he turned to Ethel who had anxiously watched the whole proceedings.

"That's all I can do at the moment. He will need careful attention for a while and really a wagon is no place for him to receive the warmth and comfort he needs."

"It's the best we can do," said Ben, "but Ethel will do all she can."

"I'm sure she will," said the doctor. "I'll be out to look at him tomorrow."

"Thanks," said Ethel. "Is it all right to move him now?"

"Not just yet, I want him to regain consciousness first."

The next half hour dragged for all those watching Mart. They had just finished a cup of coffee, which the doctor's wife had kindly made for them, when Mart stirred. The doctor and Ethel were beside him in an instant.

A faint moan came from Mart's lips. His eyes flickered, then closed again. Ethel watched anxiously.

Mart's eyes opened again. Everything was a blur. He was only aware of darker forms against a lighter background. His mind was dull as it fought against the swim of unconsciousness which threatened to take over again. He must see things clearer. He closed his eyes and opened them again but nothing had changed. Mart tried to concentrate on one of the darker objects which seemed to loom over him. His mind started to pound and everything began to whirl before his eyes. He closed them tightly. His head throbbed. As Mart opened his eyes the forms above him slowly came into focus.

"Ethel." The word was just a whisper but it brought relief and joy to her.

"Mart," she answered back.

Mart heard. He glanced at the other person and recognized the doctor.

Where was he? What had happened? Then the pain and the hurt made themselves felt. They seared through every nerve of his body and he remembered. The blacksmith's shop, the five men, the tar dripping from the brush as it came towards him.

"Doc, doc." His voice was stronger. "Am I — "

"Sure, sure." broke in the doctor, eager to reassure his patient. "You'll be all right. It will take time but you'll be all right."

Mart tried to move but winced with the pain. Then he was aware of the bandages, and he was shocked. His whole body seemed to be encased in them. Two more figures moved into view taking his attention.

"Ben, Mike," he whispered.

They both acknowledged him and Ben added, "What happened?"

"I was attacked as I went for my horse after the dance," he told them in a hesitant voice. "I was taken into the blacksmith's shop."

"The blacksmith?" gasped the doctor. "He wouldn't — "

"No," said Mart. "The door had been forced."

"Who are they?" asked Mike.

"Circle C," replied Mart.

"Circle C!" everyone gasped. They were confused. It was the last thing they expected to hear. Was Zeke Hedley turning against them? Had they mistaken the cattleman's apparent friendliness?

"You sure?" asked Ben.

"Yes."

"Did you recognize them?" asked the doctor.

"No, they had their neckerchiefs over their faces but they said they were. Mentioned the Circle C twice!"

5

THE journey back to Sundance Hollow was slow. Mike had a conscious Mart to consider. Every bump, every jerk multiplied the pain in his body but, for his sister's sake, he hid his feelings.

The rest of the nesters were glad to see them back and relieved to know that Mart was alive. They were ready with their questions but one was more important than the others, "Who did it?" They were as shocked as the gathering in the doctor's when they were told Circle C, and immediately began to wonder about their own safety.

When the wagon was in position, the horses unhitched and cared for, and Mart made as comfortable as possible, Mike called the men together.

"Now, you've all had time to think

about it, what are we going to do?" he asked, knowing that their feelings had run high against the Circle C when they first learned who had committed the atrocity. Mike hoped that in the half hour which had gone by their feelings would be tempered by clearer minds.

"I know you are all wondering why the Circle C should have done this?" said Ben. "We all thought Zeke Hedley was friendly towards us; he's fencing, he doesn't want to use Sundance Hollow but it is still open range to the cattlemen. It would seem more likely that some other outfit would try to move us on, not the Circle C." He paused. Everyone agreed with his theory. "It is difficult to believe that Zeke Hedley would do this unless forced by other cattlemen. From what we saw of him that day at the Circle C I wouldn't have thought he'd resort to this type of outrage."

Mike agreed. "I can't see Zeke being at the bottom of it."

"I think we all feel like this but there's one thing which we didn't bargain for. The day we went to the Circle C Mart took a liking to Hedley's daughter and he went to the dance hoping she would be there. Seems she was and Mart got on very well with her. No, he didn't take her home, thought it diplomatic not to as Bob Barton had taken her to the dance."

"Could have understood it if his men had tarred and feathered Mart, a sort of warning to keep off a cowboy's girl," put in Tom.

"Well, seems it was something like that," went on Ben, "but not Running W. Seems that Circle C men objected to a nester paying attention to Joan Hedley, daughter of a cattleman."

"Then Hedley himself had nothing to do with it," said Will.

"More than likely," agreed Ben.

"Nor was it directed against us as nesters," said Tom.

"Probably not," said Mike, "but

these things can have a two-fold effect. If Mart hadn't been a nester it wouldn't have happened."

"Now look here," put in Ben, "there's no need for any one of you to get involved. If you do then this can be blown into a nester-cattleman affair. Keep out of it and it could remain a private affair. I'll go and see Zeke Hedley, see what he has to say about it."

"No," put in Mike firmly. "You may be right, Ben, but one in, all in, is what I say." A murmur of agreement came from the others. "If we all stand firm together over any issue, the cattlemen will see we mean business. If you go alone Ben they might just think we don't support you."

"All right, but I don't put you under any obligation. Mart got himself into this over a girl."

"But I figure it was also meant as a lesson to us all. Zeke Hedley may not object to us but his men might. We're with you Ben. We'll pay the Circle C a visit at daybreak."

* * *

The pale light was flushing the eastern horizon when Mike and Ben rode out of their small encampment leaving Will, Tom and Jamie to take care of things in the Hollow.

They kept to a steady pace and reached the Circle C before the cowboys had ridden out to the range.

Zeke Hedley was issuing instructions to his foreman when he saw the three riders approaching. As he hurried to meet them outside his house he was aware of the grim unsmiling looks on their faces.

They exchanged brief greetings then Mike came straight to the point.

"Mart Simpson, who was here with me on the last visit, was tarred and feathered after the dance last night; claims it was your men who did it. Know anything about it?"

Mike knew the answer before it came by the look of astonishment on Zeke's face.

"No," rapped Zeke. "Did he recognize my men?"

"No."

"Then what the — " stormed Zeke before Mike could explain further, but Mike cut in Zeke's words quickly.

"They had their neckerchiefs over their faces but seems they mentioned the Circle C twice."

"What!" Zeke was astounded. He couldn't believe any of his men would do such a thing. His own friendliness towards the nesters did not seem to meet with their disapproval, unless any of them nursed a secret hate.

"Seems they were upset by Mart paying attention to your daughter at the dance," explained Ben. "Warned him about seeing her again."

Zeke was even more astonished. "I don't believe it," rapped Zeke. "My men wouldn't interfere in my daughter's private affairs, and who she sees is just that; it's no concern of any of my men."

"Well, that's Mart's story and I can't see any reason for him to make it up."

Zeke did not answer but mounted the steps to the house quickly. He opened the door and shouted for his daughter. Mike could sense the annoyance in the rancher as he stood impatiently at the top of the steps.

A moment later the door opened and Joan hurried out. She had known from the tone of her father's voice that something was wrong and when she saw the nesters she wondered what was the matter.

"Joan, have any of the Circle C men ever interfered in any way in your private affairs?"

Joan's astonishment at the question was unmistakable. "No. Why? What's the matter?"

"Mart Simpson was tarred and feathered after the dance last night." Joan gasped, her face paled. "I see you

108

did see him at the dance."

Joan nodded. "Yes," she said weakly, but then she pulled herself together and asked sharply of Mike. "How is he? Is he all right?"

"He's in a bad way but the doc says he should be all right with care and attention."

Zeke saw the relief in his daughter. "Know anything about it?" he asked.

Joan shook her head. "I had several dances with him. He left during the last waltz. I'd gone with Bob Barton and I reckon Mart was courteous enough to know that Bob would be bringing me home. But what's this about Circle C men?"

"Seems whoever did it mentioned the Circle C and warned Mart to keep away from you."

"What!" Joan was astounded. "No one runs my life." There was indignation in Joan's voice. "And I'll not have it thought that they do. Did Mart see who they were?"

"Afraid not," said Mike. "They made

sure they wouldn't be recognized; they had neckerchiefs over their faces."

Joan turned to her father. "Can we find out who they were?"

"Can try," he replied and, swinging round, he hurried towards the bunk-house.

He was back a few moments later. "Sorry, they all deny having anything to do with it; and I believe them. Wait a minute," he went on quickly halting the protestations springing to Mike's lips. "I'm just not being a boss backing his men. They had no reason to do it. According to your account Mart crossed none of my men at the dance; they've never interfered in Joan's life before and there's no reason for them to start now. I figure it was someone else using Joan as an excuse."

"But why use me?" put in Joan. "Why not just do it? Why mention the Circle C?"

"Unless someone wanted us to blame the Circle C," suggested Mike.

"You mean put you into open

conflict with us," said Zeke.

"Yes. Nearly succeeded, too, the way we all felt last night, but we waited until daylight. That gave us time to think, an' we figured that even if it was Circle C men maybe you wouldn't know anything about it."

"Just as well you didn't act hastily," said Zeke. "But who'd do this?"

"I reckon you'll be figurin' the same as us," said Ben. "The Bartons."

"But Bob was with me after the dance," Joan pointed out.

"He has men," replied Ben.

"Then I figure we ride for the Running W," said Mike.

"Hold it," Zeke halted Mike as he started to turn away. "You can prove nothin'. Go over there and you'd be stickin' your neck out. You'd ride right into big trouble. If the Running W are behind it maybe it'll suit them if you do just that."

Mike hesitated. He saw the wisdom of Zeke's words. He was right, they could prove nothing.

"So we just have to sit down and take it."

"Might be best in this case," said Zeke. "Mighty hard to do I know, but . . . well the consequences might be fatal."

"Guess you're right," said Mike. "Come on Ben, we'll get back."

The two men swung into their saddles, nodded their goodbyes and rode away from the Circle C.

"What do you think, Mike?" asked Ben as they topped the first rise and the Circle C ranch-house dropped out of sight.

Mike looked thoughtful. He had been preoccupied with his thoughts ever since leaving the house.

"I'm not sure," he replied. "There's a good case for it not being the Circle C, but can we be certain, any more than we can be certain it was someone else?"

"Well, I wasn't too happy that Hedley questioned his men without us there. How do we know that what he said was true?"

"Doesn't strike me as being that kind of a man," replied Mike.

"Yeah, but he's a cattleman," Ben reminded him. "And even if it wasn't a cattleman against nesters it could be a father not wanting his daughter to marry a nester."

"We can argue both ways and one say it was Circle C and one say it was someone else, maybe Running W, but whatever the answer we can do nothing about it now, Hedley was right about that. We'll just have to play a watchful, waiting game."

After seeing his cowboys leave for their various jobs Zeke returned to the house and it wasn't long before he detected an uneasiness in his daughter.

"Somethin' troublin' you about this affair?" he asked.

"Well . . . no . . . not exactly."

Zeke smiled. "You can't fool your old dad. Kinda like this fella Mart, don't you?"

"Well, last night was the first time I've seen him since the first time the nesters came here. Oh, he was pleasant enough and somehow I feel I might be to blame for what happened."

"What do you mean?"

"Mart broke Bob and I up in an excuse-me. Bob didn't like it but he heeded my look of no trouble. Maybe I had too many dances with Mart after that."

"Did Bob say anything?"

"That's the funny thing; apart from a couple of sarcastic remarks he said nothing, and you know Bob."

"Yes. It's unlike him not to say more."

"Well, maybe he didn't have to if he'd planned this."

Zeke nodded. "It's possible," he said thoughtfully. "Wanted to warn Mart off seeing you again."

"Why mention the Circle C?"

"Take the blame off himself, throw it elsewhere and I suppose the Circle C was an obvious choice. But we don't know that Bob was behind this, don't let's be hasty in our conclusions. It

114

might have been done to warn nesters off the open range."

"Dad, do you mind if I go to see Mart?"

Zeke was a little surprised at the request and hesitated a moment.

"If you think it best not to . . . " went on Joan.

"No, lass, no," cut in her father, "it's not that, you just took me by surprise. Sure, you ride over. Might help keep friendly relations if they're still suspicious of us."

"But I thought they were satisfied that it wasn't Circle C."

"Looked like it," agreed Zeke, "but we couldn't prove it was anyone else. I'm still a cattleman, they're nesters. The natural suspicion might be there."

"Maybe I'd better not go."

"No. You get yourself ready. Offer to help if we can but be careful, be on your guard."

It was nearly two hours later when Joan approached the wagons beside the river in Sundance Hollow. Two men were busy with some fencing a short distance away and the five women, busy with various chores beside the wagons, stopped their work and stared curiously at Joan as she rode towards them. She could feel their eyes taking in every inch of her, from her calf-length boots, across her Levis and her open-necked blouse with a neckerchief tied at her throat, to her grey sombrero hanging high on her back, by its cord around her neck. She sensed a disapproval of her dress which was in contrast to their high-necked, full length frocks with aprons tied around the waist.

"Good morning," she greeted pleasantly as she pulled her horse to a halt in front of them. "I'm Joan Hedley. I've come to see Mart Simpson."

She saw four of the women glance at the fifth who remained staring at her with unfriendly eyes and hard face. She felt the tension pulsating from this woman whom she put at about thirty.

"You can't see him and if you

want my advice you'd better leave here quick."

Joan was taken aback by the cold hostility in the tone of the voice.

"But I only want — "

"It doesn't matter what you want," the woman cut in roughly. "I'm his sister and I say you can't see him. You aren't welcome here. If it hadn't been for you this wouldn't have happened."

A young woman stepped forward. "Ethel, Miss Hedley couldn't help it; she — "

"Mart wouldn't have gone if he hadn't hoped to see her. I warned him — "

Joan was shocked by the blame she was viciously receiving. She looked down on Ethel indignantly as she steadied her horse.

"I'm sorry if you think I was to blame. I came here to enquire about Mart; I came friendly but if you don't see it that way I'll go. I should hate to upset Mart."

She turned her horse and saw that

the two men had left the fence and were hurrying towards them. Recognizing Mike and Ben she halted her horse.

"Howdy, Miss Hedley," greeted Mike amiably. "What brings you here?"

"I hoped I might see Mart," replied Joan. The two men glanced at each other. They had both sensed hurt, frustration and annoyance in her voice.

"Well, why not?" said Ben.

"She's not going near my brother!" Ethel's voice was sharp, decisive.

Ben was startled by his wife's attitude. So that was why Joan Hedley had been leaving. Ben strode past the horse.

"Now, Ethel, you've no reason to refuse," he said.

"I have. She's the cause of Mart being tarred and feathered."

"Ethel, you're carrying things to the extreme," said Ben sharply. "I know how you feel but you can't blame Miss Hedley. Your attitude won't do any of us any good. Besides you aren't your brother's keeper. For all you know

Mart might be pleased to see her."

While he was speaking Joan had swung from her horse. She came beside Ben facing Ethel.

"Please let me see him," asked Joan gently. "I came only as a friend, concerned for the man I enjoyed a number of dances with last night."

Ethel did not speak but she shifted her gaze from Joan. She hesitated, reluctant to say yes, blaming the cattlemen and their kin and not wanting to be friendly to a single one of them.

Ben stepped forward and put his arm round his wife's shoulder. "It's the best thing," he said gently.

Ethel softened a little. "All right," she said and turned away, back to her chores.

Ben smiled at Joan. "I'm sorry about that," he whispered.

"It's all right," replied Joan. "I can understand her feelings."

Ben introduced her quickly to the other women and when she shook hands with Jennie she thanked her for putting in a good word.

"That's all right," replied Jennie. "And please don't get a wrong impression of Ethel. She's a good woman whom I think you would like, it's only that she's over-wrought by what happened."

Joan was shocked by the sight of so much bandage when she climbed into the wagon but was thankful that Mart's face had been spared. He was one mass of white from his neck to his ankles. His arms were heavily bandaged and only the ends of his fingers showed.

"Hello, Mart," Joan whispered.

Mart was so surprised to see Joan that he instinctively moved. The pain shot through him from his tortured body. He winced and lay still.

"I'm sorry about this," said Joan, concern showing on her face.

Mart smiled weakly but Joan detected a sparkle in his eyes at the sight of her.

"It's nice of you to come," said Mart. "Sorry I've no better accommodation to offer you."

"That's all right," said Joan and sat on the floor of the wagon beside him.

"Ben and Mike told me they've seen your father and that they weren't Circle C men who did this."

"That's right," replied Joan.

"I wonder who?" whispered Mart. "One day I'll find out and then — "

Joan stayed ten minutes with Mart and she hoped that her visit had made him more cheerful. Mart expressed his appreciation and hoped that she would come again.

When Joan climbed out of the wagon Mike and Ben were busy repairing a wheel on another wagon. They left to join Joan when she walked over to the women who were busy near a fire preparing a meal.

"Thank you, Mrs Price, for letting me see him," she said with a smile. "Please don't think I'm interfering or criticizing if I make a suggestion." Ethel glanced curiously at her, wondering what this girl was going to say. She still felt some resentment towards her but less hostility.

"Well?" she said curtly as Joan hesitated.

"I think Mart would be better in more comfortable surroundings." Joan raised her hand to stop the indignant words she saw springing to Ethel's lips. "Now, please, before you say anything, hear me out. I know you can't help living in the wagon, you haven't had time to build a house; you've got it very nice but there isn't the comfort I feel Mart needs to help him recover quickly. It must be awkward for you and your husband. Will you let Mart come to Circle C? I can fix up a room for him and I'll give him every care possible. I don't want to take the job out of your hands so you will be welcome any time and for as long as you like."

Ethel was taken aback. She was speechless. She had not expected anything like this and, from the sincerity in Joan's voice, she knew the offer was genuine. It made her regretful of the hostility she had put out on Joan's arrival.

She looked at Ben who knew how she was feeling. "Well, what about it Ethel?" he said. "That's a mighty nice offer."

"But . . . but . . ." Ethel was lost for words. She felt ashamed of her earlier attitude. Now this girl was offering the hand of friendship even further, and yet she was the daughter of a cattleman; true, he was a cattleman who seemed more tolerant towards nesters than any they had met so far but, nevertheless, he was still a cattleman. Ethel realized Mart should have more comfortable surroundings, that it would become difficult for her and Ben having to share the same wagon, that in attending to the needs of her brother she would feel the frustration of not having the space and conveniences of a house, but she was prepared to handle things.

"I really mean it, Mrs Price. And you needn't worry, Mart will be well looked after," said Joan, trying to convince Ethel.

"And Miss Hedley said you could go over there as often as you liked," pointed out Ben. "It will be much better for Mart to be in better surroundings."

"I'm grateful, Miss Hedley," said Ethel quietly. "I'm sorry for my attitude when you arrived, but I couldn't presume on you in a case like this."

"You won't be," insisted Joan. "You said you blamed me, well I'd already had the feeling that if I hadn't been there it might not have happened, so please let me try to do something now."

"But what about your father?"

"It will be all right; I'm sure it will," said Joan.

"All right," agreed Ethel.

Joan smiled. "Come on, let's tell Mart." She held out her hand to Ethel. There was only a moment's hesitation then Ethel took it and they hurried to the wagon.

At first Mart wouldn't hear of it, thinking it an imposition on Joan and her father and that he would be a burden to them, but Joan finally convinced him that it would be more trouble to take care of him in a wagon than it would in a house.

Joan waited until the doctor called and he fully approved of the change and said it was up to Mart when he made the move but the sooner the better.

Mart said he would feel up to it that same afternoon, and, although he must have suffered agonies at times in the jolting wagon, never once did he complain. Tom accompanied Ben and Ethel and, when they arrived at the Circle C, Joan and her father, who had expressed his approval and delight at being able to help, were waiting for them.

Mart was made comfortable in the room Joan had prepared and she invited Ethel to stay if Ben would return for her during the evening.

Ethel was much happier about the whole situation when she returned to their encampment as the sun was lowering to the west sending its rays streaming along Sundance Hollow.

* * *

Bob Barton was surprised that the nesters did not hit back at the Circle C after the tar and feathering. He felt sure they would, but no word of trouble had come into town during the morning.

Curious to know what had happened Bob rode over to the Circle C in the early afternoon. He found Joan, her chores all finished, sitting on the verandah enjoying the warm Montana sun.

They exchanged greetings and Bob pulled up a chair beside her.

"Whose is the horse?" he asked nodding to the animal tied to the hitching rail beside his.

"Ethel Price's."

"Who's Ethel Price?"

"Wife of one of the nesters who've come to Sundance Hollow."

"What's she doin' here?"

"She's sister to Mart Simpson. Mart was at the dance."

"Yeah, I remember him." Bob frowned. "Hear he was tarred and feathered by some of your hands."

Joan looked hard at Bob. "Not ours. Someone seeking an excuse to assault Mart used me. Bob, you had nothing to do with it had you?"

Bob feigned surprise. "Who? Me? Why should I?"

"Well, you aren't exactly friendly towards nesters and Mart did have quite a few dances with me."

"Maybe that's so, but I don't know anything about the tar and feathering. There are plenty of other people don't like nesters. But you still haven't told me what Ethel Price is doin' here."

"She's here to see her brother."

"Her brother?" Bob looked mystified.

"We first heard about the outrage when two of the nesters rode in here yesterday morning. They were steamed up about it; thank goodness they had the sense to talk to dad rather than blowing their tops against us. Having heard about Mart I rode over to see how he was. He was in a pretty bad way and, as he couldn't get the proper care and attention in a wagon, I offered him a bed here."

"You what!" Bob was astounded. He sat upright in his chair, staring, almost disbelieving at Joan. "I came over here expecting to learn that your father had moved the nesters on, instead I hear that you've got one of them in your house. How can cattlemen hope to keep the nesters out with the likes of your father around?"

"Why don't you realize the time has come when cattlemen and nesters will have to live side by side?" rapped Joan indignantly.

"Not around here they won't. We aren't going to have nesters take away our grassland."

"There's plenty for all."

"They'll encroach, wanting more and more. Not only that, weaken to one nester and a whole lot more will come. Look what's happened in Sundance Hollow, the Nicholsons were allowed to stay, now more nesters are there, and so it will go on. We've got to be firm now and if your father isn't going to be, then we shall! I reckon I'd better have another word with him; is he around?"

"No, we're short handed so he is out with the men over on the east range, but I can tell you he has no intention of forcing the nesters out."

"What's your father thinking about?" rapped Bob irritably. "Lining himself up with nesters, desertin' his own kind."

"He's not deserting," replied Joan angrily. "He's looking farther ahead than any of you."

"Rubbish!" snapped Bob. "Nearly everyone round here sees the nesters as a menace. Your father can't be the only one who's right. If he's going to do nothing others will!"

"You won't be welcome round here then," snapped Joan.

"Seems you did take a fancy to the nester at the dance," rapped Bob jumping to his feet. "Take my advice and forget him, stick to your own kind." He swung down the steps, climbed on his horse and rode swiftly away, leaving Joan wondering if he really did know nothing about the attack on Mart.

* * *

Bob let vent to his feelings in the swiftness of his ride. Things had not developed as he had hoped after the tar and feathering but already he was formulating an idea based on a remark made by Joan.

6

TWO days later two men rode into the Circle C as the cowboys were preparing to leave for their various jobs.

"Know if your boss can use two more men?" one of them enquired.

"Better ask him, he's just comin'."

The two men turned their animals towards Zeke who was hurrying from the house to join his men. He eyed the strangers who swung from their saddles at his approach.

He saw two men with the stain of travel on them but, although their clothes showed signs of wear, they were reasonably tidy. There was nothing conspicuous about them, nothing which would draw the attention in a crowd but they both gave the impression of being able to give a good account of themselves if there was trouble.

They were well-built, strong-looking and Zeke figured they were not afraid of work and were used to an outdoor life. He put them down as drifters.

"Howdy," greeted the taller of the two. "Can you use any more men?"

Zeke eyed the two men. The one who had spoken was long faced with pointed jaw. A thin moustache covered his top lip and his dark eyes were alert. The other was more thick set with slightly lighter hair and Zeke noticed that he too had a sharp alert look in his eyes.

"Maybe. Handle cattle and horses?"

"Sure," replied the taller man.

"Done any fencing?"

"Fencin'?" The smaller man looked incredulous. "Thought this was cattle country."

"It is, but nesters are moving in, so I'm fencin' what I want before more move in."

"Wal, we ain't used to the wire," said the taller man, "but we can soon learn."

"Sure," agreed his companion.

"Right. I'll hire you Zeke Hedley's the name." He held out his hand.

The taller man took it with a grin. "Thanks. I'm Charlie Raven and this is Grant Wells."

Wells nodded and shook hands.

"Right," said Zeke, "usual rates. Find yourself a bunk. Had any breakfast?"

"Yes."

"Good. Then when you've found your bunks the foreman will detail you." As they led their horses towards the bunk-house Zeke looked their animals over. He was pleased to see they were well cared for and Zeke figured he'd been fortunate in getting these two extra men just when the pressure of work was piling up due to his fencing programme. He would not have been so pleased if he had been able to overhear the few words which passed between the two newcomers as they took their belongings into the bunk-house.

"That was easy," smiled Grant.

"Bob said if we looked the part we'd git the job," said Charlie.

"Somethin' to be said fer workin' fer two bosses," laughed Grant.

Charlie grinned. "Couple of days, then Bob wants action, that'll give us time to weigh things up."

Three days later Charlie and Grant left the Circle C for Wainwright as the evening sky was darkening, but, once out of sight of the ranch-house, they turned their mounts across the grassland and headed for the stretch of Circle C fence nearest to that part of Sundance Hollow being worked by Nicholson.

A mile from their objective they came across twenty steers which they had helped the Circle C foreman, Dusty Spraggon, segregate from the main herd that same morning. Quickly and skilfully they cut two of the steers and drove them towards the barbed wire fence which marked the limit Zeke Hedley had chosen.

While Charlie kept the steers under

control Grant quickly cut the wire until he had a hole big enough to allow the steers through.

After a couple of miles they were able to work their way on to Nicholson's land. They drove the steers to the thickets by the river and, when they had put the animals to the knife they quickly hid the carcasses in the undergrowth. As soon as they had obliterated as much of their tracks as possible they headed for Wainwright at a fast gallop; there were people there who could testify that Charlie and Grant had been there all evening if the necessity arose which they figured was most unlikely.

It was around noon the following day that Zeke, busy in one of the corrals, straightened at the sound of a galloping horse and shielded his eyes against the sun to identify the rider.

As soon as he recognized him as a Circle C rider Zeke left the corral. The swiftness of the ride meant trouble.

"Dusty says can you get over to those twenty special steers right away," shouted the rider almost before he had stopped his horse.

"What's wrong?" called Zeke anxiously, a frown creasing his weather-beaten face. Those steers were the best of his herd; if anything had happened to them someone would have to answer.

"Two missing. Wire cut," shouted the rider.

"What!" Zeke gasped and ran to the stable. He saddled his horse quickly and the two men were soon heading across the grassland at a fast gallop.

They found the foreman and three men re-checking the small herd of steers. Dusty broke away when he saw his boss approaching.

"You sure two are missin'?" asked Zeke.

"Certain, we've just checked again fer the third time," came the reply.

Zeke nodded. "Where's this hole in the wire?"

"Nearest point," answered the foreman indicating the direction.

Dusty led the way to the fence

with Zeke and the four Circle C men following.

Once Zeke had examined the hole in the wire, he called to his men. "Right, let's find 'em."

The men knew from his tone of voice and the anger on his face that there was big trouble for whoever had taken the steers.

Tracks were difficult to follow on the sunbaked ground but eventually they found themselves nearing Pete Nicholson's land. When he was certain that the steers had been taken on to the nester's land Zeke's face tightened with annoyance.

"Nesters, goddamned nesters," he hissed. "Try to help them, try to see some of it their way, try to accept them and what happens. This! This is the thanks I get!"

"Do we take Nicholson, boss?" asked the foreman.

"Let's be certain, let's find the cattle then we've got the evidence."

Two hours later after a careful search

the cowboys had failed to find the two steers. Annoyance, born of frustration, was seething in Zeke when his foreman rejoined him.

"Wal," he said, "there sure ain't any live steers around here."

"We'll git over — " Zeke stopped. "That's it," he shouted, "that's it, we're looking for live steers. If Nicholson took them he'd most likely kill and hide them."

"Only place is the thickets along the river bank," pointed out his foreman. "Unless he's got them somewhere on his wagon."

"We'll work along by the stream towards the camp," ordered Zeke.

Fifteen minutes later the dead steers were found and a grim-faced Zeke led his men at a steady trot to find Nicholson.

Smoke curled lazily from the fire above which a pot was simmering. Other belongings were still lying around but the wagon was not there.

"Wal, I guess we can wait," muttered

Zeke and swung from his saddle.

Half an hour later Pete Nicholson's wagon topped the rise above Sundance Hollow. He pulled hard on the reins halting the horses, startled by the sight of six men.

Myra glanced anxiously at her husband. "Pete," she whispered. There was no mistaking the alarm she felt.

Pete laid a reassuring hand on hers. "It's all right, honey, it's all right."

"But — " she started, only to be interrupted by Billy.

"Who are those men, Dad?"

"I don't know son. We'd better find out." He flicked the reins and sent his horses down the slope.

Fear gripped Myra when she saw the men get to their feet at the approach of the creaking wagon but that fear eased somewhat when she recognized Zeke Hedley.

"There can't be anything wrong if Hedley's here," commented Pete hoping to reassure his wife.

"But why all the men?"

"I don't know."

Myra's fear returned when she read trouble in the grim faces of the cowboys, especially in the smouldering anger in Zeke's eyes.

Pete halted the wagon and jumped down hoping to extend a friendly greeting to the owner of the Circle C, but he never got the chance.

"Nicholson, I thought I'd been fair to you. I thought this nester-cattleman problem could be solved peacefully but that meant we both had to play our part to the letter. I've tried but you, you have to take advantage of it." Zeke stared, his eyes wide with fury. "Didn't I tell you that if you wanted fresh meat to come to me? Didn't I? I'd have given you a steer. You knew that, but that wasn't good enough for you, you had to go out and kill for yourself, not one but two, not a steer that would have done but the best in my herd!"

"Hold it!" shouted Pete, angry at the accusations which had been flung

140

at him. "What the hell are you talking about?"

"Don't come the innocence with me Nicholson. We found 'em, found 'em in the thickets where you hid them."

Pete's lips tightened. "I don't know what you are talking about," he rapped.

"Two of my prize steers, brought to your land, slaughtered and hidden in the thickets by the river until you could deal with them. That's what I'm talking about Nicholson. Killin' prize steers is bad enough, but there's more to it, it proves I was wrong, proves that Barton and the others were right. I should have moved you as they said, but oh no, I was fool enough to believe that my way was the best, fool enough to trust a nester to play the game fair."

"I tell you I didn't do it," yelled Pete. His eyes swept the grim-faced cowboys, hoping for one flicker of sympathy, one glimmer of ease in the tension, but there was none. His gaze moved on to Myra still sitting in the wagon, her arms clutching her two sons tightly to her, her eyes wide with disbelief. This couldn't be happening to them. Her world, content, happy, settled only a few minutes ago was now shattered, crumbling before her. Pete saw the fear in her eyes, fear of what would happen to him and fear for the future which now held a big question-mark over it.

Pete swung round to face Zeke. "I didn't do it, can't you understand, I didn't do it." There was a pleading touch in his voice and a note of desperation. Couldn't he make them understand?

Zeke's eyes were cold as he stared at Pete. "All right, show him," he called out.

In a moment two lariats snaked out and the lassos settled neatly over Pete. Before he could do anything about them, they were pulled tight round his body. A sharp jerk sent him tumbling on the hard ground. The cowboys mounted their horses and even as Pete struggled to his feet they started to move off. As the rope tightened, Pete ran in a half stumble, trying desperately hard to keep his feet. Then he lost his balance. He hit the ground and was tumbled and twisted as the horses surged on.

"No! No!" The desperate cry came from the wagon, but it was forlorn, lost in the vengeance action of the cattlemen.

Zeke turned his horse back to the wagon. "I'm sorry this had to happen, Mrs Nicholson."

"He didn't do it. I know he didn't." The words were half a whisper and there was a plea for mercy from the tear-filled eyes.

"Were you with him all day, yesterday?" said Zeke.

"No, but — "

"Then you can't be certain."

"Pete wouldn't."

"How do you know? Why didn't he come and ask me?"

"He wouldn't beg, he's too proud."

"There was no need to beg, he

143

could have bought them everythin' — "
Zeke stopped. He stared at Myra. "He
hadn't the money to buy?"

Myra realized she had made a slip but
she could not rectify it now. She shook
her head. "No, he hadn't. Things are
a bit difficult at the moment."

"Then there's the motive. Your
husband didn't want to see you without
meat so he . . . "

"No. No. I'm sure he wouldn't."

"I'm sorry, Mrs Nicholson, all the
evidence points to your husband."
Zeke's voice hardened. "We'll be back
shortly, be packed and ready to leave
and be thankful that's all that's going
to happen. If I'd handed this over to
the sheriff your husband would be in
jail and there's no doubt about what a
cattleman jury would do." Zeke turned
his horse and galloped after his men.

By the time they reached the dead
steers Pete Nicholson was in a sorry
state. His clothes were torn and blood
oozed from several cuts and lacerations
and mingled with the dust and dirt

which covered his body after the tortuous journey at the end of the ropes. He felt a sense of relief when the tumbling stopped, and he no longer felt the hardness bruising his body. He lay gasping for breath, but his relief was short lived. Two pairs of strong arms grasped his shoulders and dragged him forward to the thickets which the other cowboys parted. He was thrust forward.

"What are those?" thundered Zeke. "Two of my best steers, slaughtered and hidden on your land."

"I know nothing about it," gasped Pete.

"Who else would hide dead steers on your land?"

"I don't know, but I didn't. Maybe I've been framed."

"Framed?" Zeke laughed harshly. "Who'd want to frame a nester? All right boys take him back."

As the strong hands released him Pete struggled to his feet but when the horses moved into a trot he could no longer keep his feet and he was dragged back to his camp.

When Myra saw the horsemen approaching she told her sons to stay near the wagon and she ran to meet the riders as they stopped close to the remains of the fire. Tears flowed at the sight of her bruised and battered husband and she fell on her knees beside him, fighting desperately to free him of the ropes.

"We'll do that ma'm." A voice boomed above her and, as one cowboy pulled her out of the way, the other quickly released the ropes. As they moved away Myra cried as she cradled her unconscious husband to her.

The thundering hooves faded leaving an uneasy stillness over the Montana countryside.

★ ★ ★

When Zeke Hedley and his men reached the Circle C, Zeke threw his reins to one of the cowboys and with a curt, "Look after him," hurried into the house.

"Joan! Joan!" he shouted as the door slammed behind him. He strode towards the kitchen but a door opened on his right and his daughter appeared. There was a questioning surprise on her face.

Zeke spun round to face her. "Get that goddamned nester out of here," he stormed.

"Dad, what's the matter?" Joan asked, anxious at the sight of the fury on her father's face.

"Get him out. I want no filthy nesters in my home."

Joan was taken completely by surprise by her father's sudden change of attitude.

"What's happened? What's Mart done?"

"Pete Nicholson stole and killed two of my best steers, two of those twenty I was telling you about."

"What! I can't believe it."

"Look, don't you start on that

attitude," snapped Zeke. "Two steers were missing, there was a hole in the fence nearest Pete's place, we found the steers on his land, dead, hidden in some thickets."

Joan was astounded. What she had seen of the Nicholsons they were a likeable family and seemed happily settled. She could hardly imagine them doing anything to jeopardize their lives.

"Did anyone see him, Dad?"

"See him! There was no need, the evidence was there."

"Couldn't someone else have done it?"

"Don't talk foolish."

"Someone tried to implicate the Circle C in the tarring and feathering."

"Joan, a nester isn't goin' to implicate another nester and no cattleman would slaughter steers as valuable as those. Now let's have no more about this, get that nester out of here, and he can tell the rest of his crowd, I expect them gone in twenty-four hours."

"But, Dad — "

"No buts," cut in Zeke roughly. "This is what I get for being tolerant to nesters, for thinkin' we could live side by side. Al Barton was right, the Nicholsons should never have been allowed to stay." He strode up the stairs leaving the protestations on Joan's lips.

Joan looked thoughtful as she returned to the room. Her father was too worked up at the moment to really think straight on this matter and she could understand it after losing two of his most prized steers. But she wondered if his attitude would be more tolerant when he had cooled down, probably not towards Nicholson but maybe towards nesters in general.

A few minutes later Joan heard her father go out and, when he returned after two hours, she detected an easing of the tension in him. She felt he was more like his tolerant self, but she resisted approaching the subject of his discontent, thinking it wiser to leave it until after they had eaten.

They had almost finished their meal

when the sound of approaching horses took Zeke to the window.

"Nesters!" he said half to himself and hurried on to the verandah to confront them. Joan left the table and joined him.

Mike led Ben, Will and Jamie right up to the verandah.

Mike nodded at Zeke. "Can we talk?" he asked civilly.

"What hev we to talk about?" asked Zeke.

"It will be easier out of these saddles," said Mike.

Zeke hesitated. "All right, climb down."

The four men swung to the ground and mounted the verandah to face Zeke.

"You gave Pete Nicholson some pretty rough treatment," Mike went on. "We — "

"You heard what he did?" cut in Zeke.

"We heard what you said he'd done," returned Mike.

"Don't quibble. The evidence was there."

"But no one saw him," put in Ben.

"Don't need to see with that sort of evidence. None of you would do it, and no cattleman would slaughter steers to implicate a nester."

"Can you be sure?" asked Mike and went on quickly without waiting to have the question answered. "Look, Mr Hedley, we don't think Nicholson did it, but nevertheless it rebounds on us, you will be suspicious of nesters, you will not be as friendly as you were."

"You're darned right I won't be. I want you out of Sundance Hollow within twenty-four hours and that nester upstairs with you."

"This is exactly what we thought would happen but we still figure you for a reasonable man, one who has a great deal of foresight in the cattleman-nester relationship, one who, when he's had time to think, won't let an incident like this cloud his judgement of the future."

151

"You're trying to bamboozle me with fancy talk, Langton." Zeke protested but deep down he knew that Mike was right. Turning off the nesters over this would not prevent others coming, the future was much bigger than this one isolated —

"Incident! This is no mere incident Langton. This is the loss of prize steers."

"We know, and we would feel the same if we were in your place," Mike went on, "but we are asking you to give us another chance. At our first meeting I judged you to be a tolerant man with a sense of fairness. It was because of that feeling that we did not ride in here with guns after Mart had been tarred and feathered. We nearly did, to have got one of your men would have satisfied, but we would have been wrong. We would have done just what someone wanted us to do."

"You are saying that this could have been another set up."

"Yes."

"Suppose it is, the question is who? You nesters wouldn't want to implicate one of your own kind, so that leaves cattlemen and I can't see a cattleman killing prize steers," Zeke pointed out once more.

Mike looked thoughtful.

"What about Al Barton?" put in Ben. "He feels strong about nesters."

Zeke smiled. "He does, but he's a cattleman, knows his cattle, thinks too much of 'em to kill senselessly."

"Even though they aren't his?"

"Yes," replied Zeke. "Al can play it rough, he can be ruthless and tough especially when it comes to nesters as you well know, but when it comes to the other cattlemen a lot of it's blow. We know him and take him as such. But I'd bet my last dollar he wouldn't deliberately kill steers."

"What about his son?"

Zeke hesitated thoughtfully.

"You don't spring to his defence immediately as you do for his father," put in Mike when he saw the hesitation.

153

"You doubt him."

"Well," mused Zeke. "I don't think he's such a cattle lover as his father. Oh, he's a cattleman, ranching will be his life but he'll never be close to cattle like Al. And he has streaks of meanness, of bravado, of wanting to appear bigger than he is. Maybe he could do it."

"There you are then," said Mike, "it's not such a closed case against Pete Nicholson."

"Maybe not," admitted Zeke a little reluctantly, "but the evidence was there. I acted on it. No, Nicholson, can't go back, but you can stay."

"Thanks, Mr Hedley," said Mike with a smile. He glanced at Ben and Will who smiled broadly and Jamie added his approval.

"Then Mart can stay here, Dad?" asked Joan, relieved that matters had been quietened down.

"All right," agreed Zeke, but his face was serious as he looked back at the nesters. "If I have one doubt, one more suspicion then it's the end; you move on."

"Right," said Mike. "Can we see Mart before we leave?"

When her father approved, Joan led the nesters into the house leaving a thoughtful Zeke toying over the nester problem.

★ ★ ★

"I hear Zeke Hedley's taken heed of our warning an' moved Nicholson out." Al Barton was pleased that Zeke had come round to his way of thinking. It was better for cattlemen to remain united in the face of a possible influx of nesters.

"Yeah," grinned Bob, "seems Nicholson killed two of his prize steers."

"What!" Al nearly exploded. "If he'd done it to mine I'd have bull-whipped him within an inch of his life. Pity about those steers," he added thoughtfully, "but I suppose it serves Zeke right, I warned him about nesters."

Bob smiled to himself. It was as well that his father didn't know he had instigated the killing. He knew his father would never approve of killing steers to achieve their ends but Bob figured if it helped what did a couple of steers matter?

"Wonder if Mr Hedley'll drive the other nesters out," said the younger Hank.

"Never you mind about that," boomed his father. "You keep your nose out of this rumpus. Sufficient time when you're a couple of years older, and by that time I figure we cattlemen will be left in peace."

"Aw, pa, I'm old enough now. I want to be with you next time you ride against nesters."

"I hope there won't be a next time. If Zeke Hedley's wise he'll have all the nesters in Sundance Hollow on the move. Bob see if you can find out if the nesters are on their way out. If not I figure we might have to give them a gentle hint ourselves."

"Sure pa." Bob grinned at his father's suggestion.

Three hours later when Bob returned, Hank and his father were watching the itinerant bronco-buster at work.

"Well?" asked Al, turning to lean his broad back against the pole-fence as Bob dropped from the saddle.

"Nesters ain't movin'" said Bob, annoyance showing on his face. "Nicholson moved all right. Zeke saw to that. Gave him some rough treatment. Nicholson went to the other nesters who sent a deputation to see Zeke. Seems Zeke was goin' to move them all but they talked him into lettin' them stay."

Al cursed. "That cattle killin' could have worked in our favour. Wal I reckon we'll work something out to give them damned nesters a prod on their way tomorrow."

"Can I come?" asked Hank, excitement showing in his eyes at the prospect of riding alongside his father and brother.

"No," rapped Al.

"Aw, pa," Hank groaned.

"You ain't a man yet," said Al.

"But — " Hank started.

"Quiet, little brother," grinned Bob, "it won't be kid's stuff tomorrow." He turned and led his horse away.

Hank glanced at his father but he saw the rancher's attention going back to the bronco-buster and knew it was useless to say more. He left the fence and wandered in a thoughtful mood towards the stables.

Hank saddled his horse slowly and left the ranch at a steady trot. He rode nowhere in particular, his thoughts occupied with his father's refusal to let him participate in running the nesters out of this country. He knew the reason well enough, his pa was thinking of his mother. Trouble could result in death and as long as one son was at home his ma would never be alone if the worst happened. But why was it always him? Hank wanted treating as a man, wanted to share in all men's

158

work. If his pa wouldn't let him ride with him then he'd have to ride alone. He'd prove himself, then they'd have to take notice and include him and that smart-alec, his brother, would have to forget the kid stuff. By the time Hank returned to the ranch he knew exactly what he was going to do.

After the evening meal Hank made his excuses and in a few minutes was hurrying quietly in the gathering darkness to the stables. He quickly saddled a horse but, before leading it from the stables, he found some rags, weighted them at one end with stones, soaked them in oil from the lamp supply and put them in his saddle-bag. He led his horse from the stable, pausing at the door to make sure no one was about. Noise came from the bunk-house and lights streamed from the windows of the ranch-house but there was no one outside. He led the animal quickly away from the buildings and waited until he had got about a quarter of a mile before mounting.

Hank kept it to a walking pace until he reckoned he was out of ear-shot of the ranch. Then he put the horse into a trot through the Montana darkness.

Hank kept it to a steady pace, heading for Sundance Hollow. The night was fine and clear, and, knowing the countryside, he had no difficulty in judging his ride to bring him to the edge of Sundance Hollow a little to the west of the nesters' encampment. He slipped from the saddle and, from the top of the hill, saw the flickering fires light up the wagons beside the river. He could make out the horses picketed on the west side of the wagons.

Hank moved swiftly to his horse, secured it for his return and removed the oil-soaked rags from his saddlebag. Swiftly and silently he moved down the hillside, carefully watching the people around the fires. He kept well to the right of the horses not wanting to create a disturbance yet. Once he was between the river and the animals he moved swiftly towards them. They stirred, but a soothing whisper quietened them and reassured them as he moved swiftly away among them releasing them from their pickets. When he had completed his task, he glanced anxiously towards the fires, but all was normal, no one had noticed anything untoward.

Hank paused, weighing up his line of action, then, satisfied, he slapped the nearest horse on the rump turning it in on the other animals. Startled they all turned away from the disturbance. Hank moved quickly after them slapping the nearest ones hard and letting out a scaring yell. The animals panicked and broke into a gallop away from the noise.

As soon as he yelled Hank ran swiftly towards the stream and made for the thickets close to the nearest wagon.

Pandemonium had broken out in the camp at the disturbance.

"It's the horses!"

"Someone's at the horses!"

"Get after them!"

The nesters raced after the animals.

Hank grinned. He fumbled in his pocket found some matches and quickly applied a flame to one of the rags. Grasping the stone-weighted end he hurled it to fall on the nearest wagon. He watched, saw the flame increase and then moved until he was opposite the next wagon, which received the same treatment.

At the sight of the flames springing from their wagons the women ran to try to do something yelling to their men folk. Men yelled instructions and advice to each other as they turned from their first object of trying to retrieve the horses, to trying to quell the flames which, taking a hold on the wagons, sprang towards the black Montana sky.

Hank, making his way to the next wagon, was pleased. He stopped and looked back as the flames flared, devouring the wagons and their contents. He was fascinated by the destruction. Maybe the nesters would now realize that it would be better to move on. Maybe now that he had proved himself his father would let him ride with him.

Suddenly Hank realized his danger. The men were back at the wagons. He'd better clear out. He crept along beside the river until he judged he should be safe enough to swing round the camp and make for his horse. He started to leave the thickets when a blow pounded into the middle of his back pitching him head first on to the ground. Hank heard the yell of, "I've got him! Over here!" and before he could twist over someone fell on to his back pinning him to the ground.

Try as he would Hank could not shift the weight which held him, pressing his face into the hard ground and pinning his arms so that he could not move.

Voices came nearer.

"Where are you?"

"Over here!"

"Who is it?"

A few moments later feet stopped beside him. He felt the weight on him ease to be replaced by strong hands which yanked him unceremoniously to his feet. He was gripped by two men whose faces left no doubt as to what they would do.

7

FLAMES, leaping towards the night sky, cast dancing shadows across the nester encampment. They lit the grim faces of Mike Langton and Will King as they faced their captive. Ben Price and Tom Byron held him tightly forcing him on in no gentle manner. Jamie strode beside him pleased that he had caught the fire-raiser.

The women stood to one side, gazing helplessly at the flaming wagons, which blazed so furiously that nothing could be done to save them or their belongings.

"Jamie got him," said Tom when they reached Mike and Will.

"Good lad, Jamie," congratulated Mike.

"I figured he'd move in the opposite direction to the horses after he'd fired the wagons. I reckoned he'd think he'd be safe that way with everyone's attention on the horses and wagons."

"Good thinkin', lad," said Will. "Who is he? Anyone know him?"

They peered at the dishevelled figure, his face dirty where Jamie had pushed it into the ground. Ben and Tom turned him so that his face was lit by the flickering flames but no one recognized him.

"We'll soon find out," rapped Mike, his temper which was already near boiling point still rising as the noise of the crackling fires bit deeper into his brain. He glanced at his companions and knew they held no compassion for this youngster who had caused the destruction.

"Who are you?" rapped Mike peering hard at Hank.

Hank said nothing. His lips were set in a defiant line and he met Mike's gaze. But Mike detected the fear which lay behind the steady eyes and defiant look. He figured these were outward signs of bravado, of a false courage worn by someone who had taken on something which he had suddenly found bigger than himself. Mike figured he could break him.

Suddenly, without any warning, Mike sank his fist deep into Hank's stomach. Hank gasped; he started to double up but Ben and Tom jerked him upright holding him stiff so that no relief could come from the closing of his body. One more blow sank viciously into his stomach. Hank cried out as the pain shot through him.

"Who are you?" snarled Mike.

Still no answer.

Mike's control was disappearing fast. He swept the back of his hand hard across Hank's face. His head jerked sideways but was immediately driven back by another blow. Mike aimed again but Will stopped him.

"Steady, Mike. He's only a youngster, no older than Jamie."

Mike's eyes glared. "We want to know who he is, who ordered him here." He hit Hank again.

Hank's face grimaced in pain. His brain pounded. What would these men do to him? He had never felt hurt like this before. Would it never stop? Why had he come? What would his father say? Why hadn't he left this to him? His pa had told him to do so. Through glazed eyes he saw another blow coming. He couldn't stand another!

"Hank . . . Hank Barton," he gasped.

Mike stopped his blow. "Barton!" he whispered. "Al Barton's son?"

Hank nodded weakly.

"Then he'll have to be taught another lesson," said Mike. "Tie him to the wheel of the wagon."

"Remember what Hedley said," Jamie reminded him.

"This isn't Hedley's doing. He couldn't expect us to take what's happened here tonight and not do anything about it."

"He said, 'Any trouble', and we'd have to move," pointed out Will.

"But this has nothing to do with the Circle C, Barton must be warned, and what better way than through his son."

The women had closed with the fire-lit group.

"Mike, please, no more. Remember what happened last time." Jennie put in a word. "Retaliation might be worse this time, he's no older than Jamie."

Mike hesitated. He glanced round the grim faces of the other nesters but he did not see there a determination for revenge, only a weariness that trouble could be flaring up all over again. Maybe they were right, maybe he should leave things as they were. Barton's son was hurt, that could be enough.

"All right," said Mike, "let him go."

Ben and Tom released their grip. Hank's knees began to buckle but he forced himself to stay on his feet. His head felt dull and heavy but he was determined not to show his feelings to these nesters. He could hardly believe they were letting him go. They must be afraid of the consequences; maybe he had won after all, maybe they would move on, afraid of what Al Barton would do after seeing his son.

He glanced round the faces, shadowed by the dying flames. Without a word he turned and forced himself to walk into the darkness.

Every movement sent pain searing through his body but, fighting it, he kept walking until he was beyond the tell-tale light. He staggered a few more yards then sank to the ground enjoying, in spite of the hurt, the relief he found in the relaxation of support for his body. How long he lay there he never knew but slowly some of the pain subsided and his head cleared. When he felt sufficiently recovered he pushed himself to his feet and started off towards the dark mass of the hillside. He staggered his way to the slope, his hands holding his stomach from which the pain had disappeared leaving a bruised hurt which made itself felt with every step.

Hank moved slowly up the slope. It seemed he would never reach the top but he forced his weary body on. Then he topped the hillside and found he was only a few yards from his horse. He staggered to the animal and, on the third attempt, managed to get into the saddle. He turned the horse towards the Running W and, as the horse set off, Hank slumped forward in the saddle only just managing to keep sufficient of his senses to hold on. Slowly but steadily the horse, with its tortured rider, moved across the Montana grassland.

Hank was unaware how long the ride took him, most of it had been in a daze, with his head reeling from his beating and his blurred thoughts wondering what his father would say.

He reached the ranch just as two cowboys were riding in from town. Surprised to see a rider slumped in the saddle, they ranged their horses alongside and were even more surprised to find it was the boss's younger son in a beaten condition.

Taking charge of Hank's horse, they led it as quickly as they dare to the ranch-house and soon roused the Bartons from the quietness of their front room.

"What the — " gasped Al when he saw Hank supported by two of his ranch-hands standing in the doorway.

"Just found him riding in, slumped in the saddle," explained one of the men.

"Bring him in, bring him in," blustered Al, stepping to one side. He was about to shout to his wife but she had already come to the room door to see what all the commotion was about.

When she saw her son being helped in by two men her face paled and she ran forward. "Hank! Oh! Hank!" She stopped in front of her son her hands reaching gently to examine his lacerated face.

He smiled wanly. "I'll be all right, ma." Meg glanced anxiously at her husband and then taking a grip on herself, she was in command of the situation. This was no time to give way to her feelings. Her son needed her, needed a mother but a mother who was able and efficient, bringing relief to his battered body.

"Bring him upstairs," she ordered and led the way up the stairs to Hank's bedroom where she had the bedclothes turned back by the time the two men arrived with Hank. They eased him on to the bed and after they had left Al came to the bedside to help his wife with Hank's clothes.

"What happened son?" asked Al.

Hank hesitated, wincing as his shirt was peeled off. Meg gasped when she saw the ugly bruises on Hank's stomach and ribs and glanced anxiously at Al, who had been taken as unawares at the unexpected that he was speechless for a moment.

"Who did this?" he asked, his voice

quiet but not disguising what he felt towards his son's attackers.

"The nesters, pa."

"What!" Al's voice rose. Anger and hate stormed across his face.

Meg was about to say something but she stopped herself. This was man's business and no amount of talk on her part would persuade her husband otherwise. She kept silent and went about ministering to the needs of her son quietly and efficiently.

"Where was this? What happened?"

"Pa, you wouldn't let me ride with you tomorrow. I wanted to prove myself so I went over to the nesters' camp." Hank went on to relate what had happened and Al listened without interrupting.

Al looked at Hank when his son had finished. "There was no need to try to prove yourself, Hank. I know that you're capable of being part of these things, you're more than good with cattle and horses, you have that flare, that little something that Bob hasn't

174

got. Maybe it's a feeling for them, well whatever it is, when you're as good as you are I know you'd handle yourself well in any situation, same as you have tonight. Mistake you made was getting caught. But I had a reason for not taking you tomorrow; I was thinking of your ma. If anythin' went wrong, if anythin' happened to me and Bob your ma would have someone left."

Hank nodded. "Sorry, pa, if I messed things up."

"You haven't," replied Al. "Maybe you've let the nesters see they aren't wanted, maybe they'll realize we won't leave them alone. In any case it gives me the best excuse to prod them."

Meg looked at her husband, alarm on her face. "Al, no, you — "

"Meg, no man beats my son and gets away with it." Without waiting for a reply he swung out of the room, hurried downstairs, fastened on his gun-belt and left the house.

He walked quickly towards the bunk-house but before he reached it Bob and

175

the Running W foreman rode in from town. As they turned towards the stable Al shouted, "Bob, Luke, stay in those saddles we're ridin'!"

Before Bob could turn his horse to find out what was the matter his father had entered the bunk-house and was instructing the five men he found there to saddle up. Bob knew from his father's tone that something bad had happened, and it must be mighty important to be riding at this time of night.

Bob jumped from the saddle outside the stable and was already saddling his father's horse when Al came into the building.

"What's happened?" queried Bob as he cinched the saddle tighter.

"Hank was beaten up by the nesters," replied Al.

"What!" Bob was surprised. "How did this happen?"

"Wanted to prove he was fit to ride with us so he headed out after we'd eaten. Set fire to a couple of the

176

nesters' wagons."

"Did he!" Bob expressed his surprise again. "Good fer little brother."

"Yeah, but he made the mistake of gettin' caught."

"What do you figure on doin', pa; blastin' them nesters out?" asked Bob.

"That's what they might expect; they might be ready for us. I figure on takin' the nester who won't be expectin' us."

"You mean Mart Simpson at the Circle C?"

"Yeah. Show them damned nesters another lesson in the right place and they'll maybe take it to heart this time."

"You figurin' Zeke will resist?" asked Bob indicating the men who were saddling their horses.

"You never know with Zeke. A show of strength might just swing the scales. I'll be surprised if he condones a cattleman's son being beaten up." He glanced around the dimly lit stable. "Everybody ready?" he shouted.

The Running W men moved out of

the stable and a few minutes later the thunder of the hooves sent a chill into a woman's heart as she tended her beaten son.

Al made the ride fast and spread the word among the men about the purpose of their mission.

Hooves thrummed and lacerated the Montana earth as the horses pounded towards the Circle C. The rumble which grew louder as the Running W riders thundered closer and closer to the ranch-house brought Zeke and Joan hurrying on to the verandah to see what it was all about. Light streamed from the bunk-house door as cowboys hastened to satisfy their curiosity.

Joan glanced anxiously at her father as the eight riders emerged out of the darkness. There was no mistaking the bulky silhouette of Al Barton. As they pulled to a halt in front of the verandah, the lights from the ranch-house windows revealed the grim faces.

"What's on, Al?" called Zeke determined to get the first word in.

"Those goddamned nesters beat up Hank tonight."

"What!" Zeke gasped and cursed the nesters to himself. Now there would be trouble. His face darkened, and Joan glanced at her father in alarm, "How did it happen?" asked Zeke, wondering why Al was here when he would have expected him to have been riding hard for the nesters' camp.

Al explained the situation briefly and sharply. "Now, we want that nester you have in your house."

Zeke felt the alarm in his daughter as she grasped his arm.

"He had nothing to do with it," Zeke pointed out.

"He's a nester, use him again and the nesters might see sense and move on. Ride on their camp, there might be bloodshed, they could be expecting us. We'll take the easy one, Zeke."

Zeke's face was grim. "Sorry, you won't."

Al frowned, "You sidin' with these nesters after what they've done to my son?" boomed Al. "Don't get in my way Zeke."

"Don't threaten me," rapped back Zeke. "I don't condone what the nesters have done and maybe I'd do just what you're doin' but takin' Simpson is no answer to it."

"We'll soon see," snapped Bob.

"Keep out of this, Bob," shot back Zeke sharply, "it's between your pa and me. Don't you try to stir up more trouble." He turned his attention back to Al. "I'll say it again, takin' Simpson is no answer. I warned those nesters yesterday that if there was any more trouble they'd have to move. All right, they may have had cause to retaliate, you and I probably would have done the same in the heat of the moment, but after my warnin' they shouldn't have retaliated. I'm a cattleman at heart and I'll not stand by and see the son of my friend suffer without something being done about it."

"Now you're talkin'," said Al pleased

that Zeke was now seeing things his way.

"Pa!" There was protestation in Joan's voice.

Zeke felt her grip on his arm tighten. He patted her hand reassuringly and then went on. "But you don't get Simpson! He's innocent of this."

"Then you'll drive us into bloodshed," pointed out Al. "That's what'll happen if you force us to ride on that nester camp."

"I'm not forcin' you to do anythin'," shot back Zeke. "Get the men who did the actual beating but not by riding in there yourselves. Get the law out, make it an official arrest. Maybe they were provoked by Hank, but you know as well as I do that they'll be found guilty by a cattlemen jury. That way no blood will be spilt."

"Don't listen to him, pa. I say ride in and get 'em now. Let's finish them once and for all."

"Do that," lashed Zeke. "Maybe get some of these men killed, maybe you, maybe your father. Al, you don't want that if there's another way."

"Don't listen, pa," shouted Bob. "Next thing he'll be lettin' those nesters stay on."

"He makes sense, Bob," shouted Al. "No sense in anyone gettin' killed if it can be avoided." He looked hard at Zeke. "You said you'd move 'em on if there was any more trouble?"

"Yes," Zeke replied. "They'll be told tomorrow thet they'll hev to move as soon as the trial's over and Simpson can move and I figure that they'll be movin' within a week."

"Pa — " Bob started to protest again but he was interrupted by his father.

"You'll keep to that, Zeke?"

"Sure. You'll be there to witness it. I'll meet you at the sheriff's office in the morning and we'll all ride out together."

"All right," agreed Al. "We'll both take some men along. Let the nesters see strength as a warning what will happen if they don't move."

"Right, nine o'clock in Wainwright."

"Fine. See you." Al turned his horse quelling the protestations which sprang to Bob's lips.

Zeke turned and walked slowly into the house as the sound of hooves faded into the darkness.

"Is this really the end of the nesters, pa?" asked Joan, as she closed the door.

"I don't know. I played for time. I hope I've got it. Tomorrow I'll have to tell them to move and they'll see what will happen if they don't, but waitin' for the trial and for Mart may just give time for somethin' to turn up." He paused, then added thoughtfully, "So long as nobody else does anything foolish."

The three men whom Zeke took with him the next morning included Charlie Raven and Grant Wells but they showed no sign of knowing Bob when they joined the Running W men outside the sheriff's office in Wainwright.

Zeke found Al explaining what had

183

happened to Sheriff Chris Lever. "Hank says it was Langton who beat him. I reckon if you arrest him, sheriff, it ought to be good enough, he appears to be the leader of the nesters."

"Right," said the sheriff, only too pleased to see a possible end to the nester problem without the big trouble which had promised to flare up.

A few minutes later twelve riders were heading for Sundance Hollow at a steady pace.

Jennie Langton was the first to see the riders top the rise and spill down the slope in the direction of the camp.

"Mike!"

Her husband who was examining the burnt out wagons for any possible salvage sensed the alarm in her shout.

He looked in her direction to see her directing his attention to the hillside. He stiffened at the sight of the horsemen then hurried to his wife's side. The other nesters who had also heard the shout and had seen the riders, joined them. There was alarm and fear at the sight of the approaching men. The thunder of the hooves beat that fear into them. There was no mistaking the purposeful determination of that ride and not one nester was under any delusion as to what it was all about when they saw the Bartons to the fore. The only one relieving factor was that Zeke Hedley was with the party.

The nesters waited silently as the riders approached and halted a few yards in front of them. The cowboys ranged themselves in a line, their hands close to their Colts. They were alert, ready for action, their eyes never leaving the nesters who realized they were in a hopeless position.

The sheriff swung out of the saddle and stepped forward.

"Langton, you're under arrest for the brutal beating of Hank Barton."

"Oh, no!" Jennie's thoughts went wild as she clung to her husband's arm. What would happen to him? He would have to face a cattlemen jury. He was guilty already. But, even in the troubling questions and conclusions, one thing struck Jennie, the cattlemen had not ridden in bent on brutal revenge. She had feared Al Barton would mete out his own punishment as he did in Sioux Hollow. Instead he was here with the law and that meant a certain degree of safety for Mike.

Mike met his accuser's gaze squarely. "What about our wagons? Will Hank Barton stand trial for destroying those?"

"Git your horse," replied the sheriff.

Mike hesitated waiting for an answer to his question. It did not come but he knew the answer in the silence.

"Get my horse, Jamie, please," he said. Jamie hesitated. "Go on, Jamie. We can't do anything, it's best if I go quietly."

Jamie hurried to get the horse.

"I'm sorry about this, Langton," called out Zeke, "but I did warn you that if there was any more trouble you'd have to move." He eyed Nicholson. "You were already told to move out, see that you do this time."

186

Mike, obviously surprised at the inference, stared at the rancher. "But we didn't cause the trouble, young Barton did, there's the evidence." Angrily he pointed at the burnt out wagons. "You can't mean we have to move because of this."

"Sorry," replied Zeke firmly. "As soon as your trial's over and Mart fit to move then you'll have to go."

"But — " started Mike as the anger swelled inside him. He stopped and then went on. "Oh, what's the use. We're on a loser." He looked hard at Zeke. "I thought we had a hope with your friendship, but I might have known you were a cattleman and couldn't change."

The contempt in Mike's voice hurt Zeke. If only he could tell him he was doing it to save bloodshed and that he was hoping to buy time for something to work out, that Al Barton would not have hesitated to use his guns.

Jamie returned with the horse and, after bidding Jennie not to worry, Mike climbed into the saddle and rode beside the sheriff. As the cowboys turned their horses. Bob moved purposely through Jennie's line of vision as she watched her husband riding away. Bob's eyes met hers and he grinned back at the hateful look she gave him.

Half-way to Wainwright the men from the ranches parted to return to their own spreads, except for Bob Barton, who on his own suggestion, assisted Sheriff Lever in escorting Mike to town.

After the posse had ridden out of Wainwright rumour had spread quickly through the town and talk against the nesters was rife. There were plenty of people about when the sheriff and Bob Barton rode in with Mike. Abuse was flung against the nesters from the gathering outside the sheriff's office as the riders pulled to a halt.

The sheriff slipped quickly from the saddle and was beside Mike as he swung to the ground. With Bob beside him they shouldered their way through the crowd, angered at the sight of the man who beat up young Barton. The sheriff was relieved when they got inside the office and he had Mike behind bars.

"Glad you came along, Bob. Thanks for your help," said Lever as he sat down behind his desk. "Pleased we aren't bringing Langton in on a murder charge, that lot outside could have got lynch fever."

"Want me to stay around?" asked Bob.

"I reckon it'll be all right now," said the sheriff. "If they don't disperse I'll move 'em on."

Bob crossed to the window. "They're beginning to drift," he called over his shoulder, but there were still one or two people hanging about when he left the office a few minutes later.

As he crossed the street to the saloon, Bob sensed that the feelings of the people could be roused further against Langton and the nesters. If they moved on as they had been told all well and good but if things eased for them this was a useful idea to have. Bob was still suspicious of Zeke Hedley, he felt the rancher had come round too easily to Al's way and if he had some plan for helping the nesters to stay then Bob planned to play on the feelings he had witnessed today.

During the next three days Bob was active moving around the countryside and paying frequent visits to Wainwright. He was determined to keep an eye on things, to make sure the nesters moved out once and for all, that Zeke didn't soften and agree to giving the nesters another chance.

Bob saw the preparations for leaving were going along slowly as the nesters waited for Mike's trial. He sounded out Zeke, who gave nothing away, and he briefed Charlie Raven and Grant Wells to be ready for instant action should he require it.

Feelings in Wainwright still simmered against the nesters and Bob, with the help of Raven and Wells kept them that way with talk and rumour.

During the afternoon of the third day after Mike's arrest Bob rode to the Circle C to see Joan. He found her alone on the verandah.

Her greeting was pleasant but when Bob asked her to go with him to the next dance in a week's time she refused.

"But why, Joan?" he asked. "We've always — "

"Not after what happened last time," cut in Joan.

"But that was nothing," laughed Bob. "There'll be no nester there this time."

"Besides," went on Joan, "Mart is still a guest in this house and I'm not going to — "

"You're gettin' boggle-minded about nesters," snapped Bob irritably. "Time Simpson was on his way like the rest of them."

"Maybe he won't be leaving."

"What do you mean?" asked Bob, suspicion lurking in his mind.

"Nothing," replied Joan.

"You gettin' stuck on him?"

"Could be," answered Joan with an irritating lilt to her voice which roused Bob's anger.

"You prefer a lousy nester to me? I thought you and I were — "

"You shouldn't jump to conclusions," cut in Joan. "I know we've seen a lot of each other, growing up together but I don't think I ever gave you cause to regard it as anything more than a close friendship. If you took it any other way I'm sorry."

Bob's lips tightened. Anger rose against Mart whom Bob blamed for Joan's change of attitude which he reckoned had come about even though she said she had never felt any different towards him.

"Damned nesters!" hissed Bob as his anger flared. "Cause of all the trouble. Now one has come between you and me. I should have more than tarred and feathered him. I won't — "

He stopped, realizing he had said too

much, the words which he had never meant to say had slipped out in his anger. And he knew by the incredulous look on Joan's face that she had not missed them.

"You had Mart tarred and feathered!" gasped Joan. She felt numb as the meaning bit into her mind. "You danced with me planning that outrage and tried to put the blame on Circle C men!"

"He deserved it!"

"No man deserved the torture Mart has gone through. He was out for the first time yesterday and it will be at least a week before he'll be better."

"We had to get those damned nesters out and your pa wouldn't see it that way. Thank goodness he has now but it's taken some working to get him to see sense."

"Don't be too sure you've succeeded," snapped Joan. She didn't know whether her father would reverse his decision but in her anger at Bob she made the statement to annoy him.

"Your pa had better not change his mind," lashed Bob, "or else I'll — "

"Don't you threaten my father, nor me," said Joan her eyes flashing angrily. "The sooner you leave the better."

Bob glanced at her, was about to say something but changed his mind. He swung on his heels and a few moments later was galloping away from the Circle C, his mind angered even more against the nesters.

8

JOAN felt shock and anger as she watched Bob Barton ride away and she was not aware that her father had come out of the house until he put a comforting arm round her shoulders.

"I was in my room, the window was open, I couldn't help overhearing," said Zeke.

"You heard, Bob was responsible for Mart?"

Zeke nodded. "I did. I also wonder what he meant when he said that it had taken some workin' to get me to see sense about the nesters." Joan glanced questioningly at her father. "If Bob was responsible for the tarring," went on Zeke, "could he have been behind the slaughterin' of those two steers?"

"And then hiding them on Pete Nicholson's land knowing that the broken wire fence would lead a search

195

that way," added Joan.

"Nicholson protested his innocence all the time. Was I wrong in condemning him?" Zeke looked worried.

"You only moved those steers nearer to Nicholson's land that day. Nicholson could have seen them but Bob wouldn't know about them," pointed out Joan.

"You're right," agreed her father, "but supposin' Bob bribed one of my men to inform him when there was a chance of doin' somethin' which might put me against the nesters."

Joan's eyes brightened. "He could, but I don't think any of our men would — " She stopped, excitement danced in her eyes. "You signed on two new men about that time, Dad."

"Charlie Raven and Grant Wells!" exclaimed Zeke. "Bob could have planted them." He paused thoughtfully. "But I hadn't put it around that I wanted more men. The situation only arose because I was fencin', I was willin' to take some on if they happened to come in, but I hadn't mentioned it to anyone, Bob could only surmise I wanted men, hardly a sound basis for wantin' or tryin' to plant a couple of men here."

"No, I suppose not," said Joan, "but — " She stopped and looked excitedly at her father. "Bob knew! He came looking for you one day, I remember now, you were out with the men. I told him you were helping because we were short-handed."

"So he could have planted them!" said Zeke.

"Get rid of them, Dad," urged Joan.

"No, I'll tell Dusty to keep his eyes on them. We need some evidence. Besides if I get rid of them it might put Bob on his guard." Zeke started down the verandah steps to seek his foreman but he stopped, turned round and looked hard at his daughter. "You think a lot about Mart." It was half a statement half a question.

"More than I do about Bob Barton."

★ ★ ★

Jennie pulled her horse to a halt outside the sheriff's office. She smiled reassuringly at Jamie as he pulled alongside. They had both sensed the hostility in the curious stares as they had ridden along the main street of Wainwright. It had been the same each day they had visited Mike but today Jennie felt the tension all the more. She had expected that feelings would cool with the passage of time but it was not so, it was as if someone was keeping things on the boil.

Brother and sister swung from their saddles and, after hitching their horses to the rail, climbed the four steps on to the sidewalk and entered the sheriff's office. Chris Lever made no comment as he pushed himself out of his chair, took down a bunch of keys from a hook beside the door to the cells and unlocked it. He pushed it open and returned to his seat.

Jennie thanked him and went into the cell block, accompanied by Jamie. There were three cells on either side of the block but only one was occupied.

Mike jumped off the bed when he saw Jennie and Jamie and greeted them with a warm smile. He took his wife's hands between the bars and they kissed as best they could.

"Hi, sheriff," he called. "Have a heart let my wife sit down." There was silence. "Sheriff!" Mike shouted again. "I thought you men in this part of the country respected your womenfolk."

They heard the chair scrape and a moment later the sheriff appeared with the bunch of keys. He unlocked the cell door without a word, Jennie went into the cell but Jamie waited. The sheriff looked quizzically at him.

"You goin' in?" he asked.

"No. They'll want to be alone," replied Jamie.

The sheriff shrugged his shoulders, relocked the cell door and returned to his office.

"Thanks, sheriff," called Mike. He turned to his wife, held her tightly for a few moments and then let her sit down on his bed. Mike wanted to know all the news from the encampment.

"We're worried," said Jennie, concern in her eyes. "Hostility is building up."

"Has anything else happened?" asked Mike, a worried frown creasing his brow.

"No, but you can feel it when you come into town."

"You certainly can," confirmed Jamie. "It seemed worse today. Ben, Tom, Will and Pete Nicholson came into town for supplies yesterday and they felt it. Reckoned the storeman was rough on them price-wise."

"They called to see you," added Jennie, "but the sheriff wouldn't let them in. Only Jamie and I are allowed to see you."

"We don't like this tension, Mike," said Jamie.

Jennie looked at her brother and nodded in the direction of the sheriff's office. Jamie acknowledged her nod and strolled out of the cell block into

200

the sheriff's office.

"Mind if I wait in here, sheriff?" he asked. "Let them be alone for a few minutes."

"Suit yourself," said Lever, and returned his attention to the wanted posters he had on his desk.

"Thinking of a few rewards?" asked Jamie. He had touched on a pet subject of the sheriff's and Jennie was pleased when she heard the drone of conversation coming from the office. She knew Jamie had the sheriff occupied.

Mike had noticed the exchanged signal between sister and brother but he made no comment knowing he would be told what it was all about in due course.

When Jennie was sure the sheriff was occupied she changed the topic of conversation. "Mike, we all know that the verdict will go against you. Tension is high in town. We — "

"But I had cause Jennie. Any cattleman would have done the same if he'd caught the person who'd burnt his wagons. If they try me they'll have to try young Barton."

"They should but they won't," said Jennie.

"If I push it hard about Hank Barton they'll have to. If not they'll have to set me free. This could be a test case for homesteaders."

"Mike, it's no use setting yourself up like this. This is your trial, you're in a cattle-town, will be tried by cattlemen. You won't be able to force anything. You'll be convicted and that will be that. Feelings are running high, all of us feel it."

"It can't be as bad as that, Jennie," said Mike trying to ease the agitation he saw in his wife.

"Believe me it is, Mike," said Jennie forcibly. "It's just as if someone was keeping the feeling against us on the boil. If you were on a murder charge a lynch mob would have been yelling for your blood and maybe getting it."

Mike could see the earnestness in his

wife. "But what can I do about it in here?"

"We'll get you out. Everyone's in agreement that it should be done."

"No. Jennie it will only lead to more trouble," replied Mike firmly, after he had recovered from the immediate shock at the suggestion. "There could be shooting if things went wrong and that might mean killing. I'm grateful to everyone, but it's too risky. It will make them wanted men."

"They know all this but they are prepared to take the risk. We all realize that we'll have to leave here but we are all prepared to do that. Ben figures that the only pursuit will be as far as our camp; once the cattlemen see we've gone they won't bother to come after us, they will have got what they wanted. But the men won't act unless you agree."

Mike looked thoughtful for a few moments, then he looked at Jennie. "What do you want?" he asked.

"I want you back with me, not in

jail. I think as Ben does, if we get away nobody will come after us. I'd rather that than see you go to jail."

"In spite of the risk?"

"Yes," replied Jennie. "But that will be slight; nobody will expect a jail break."

"All right," agreed Mike. "What's the plan?"

"Just you be ready for whatever happens," replied Jennie, relieved that Mike had agreed. "I'll go to the Circle C to let Mart know we'll be pulling out, and Jamie will let the men know you agree."

A few moments later Mike called to the sheriff to let Jennie out of the cell. They said goodbye and Jennie and Jamie left the sheriff's office.

★ ★ ★

After leaving the Circle C Bob kept his horse to a fast gallop working off some of his fury in the speed of the ride but anger directed at the nesters still seethed through him when he hit Wainwright. He pulled to a halt in front of the saloon and, after hitching his horse to the rail, he hurried inside. He bought his beer and took it to a table near the bar.

Six beers later he stiffened in his chair when he saw Jennie Langton and her brother come out of the sheriff's office. He watched her as they paused on the sidewalk and exchanged a few brief words. Jamie nodded and, leaving his sister, climbed on his horse and rode out of Wainwright. Jennie watched him for a moment and then walked to the store unaware that eyes were admiring her figure smartly clad in open-neck blouse and split riding skirt, which reached to the top of black riding boots.

Bob finished his beer and waited to see Jennie come out of the store. A few moments later she appeared and hurried to her horse outside the sheriff's office. As she rode slowly along the main street Bob left the saloon, unhitched his horse and followed.

Leaving Wainwright, Bob checked his pace to match Jennie's while keeping at a distance which would not attract her attention. His mind prodded by the beer raced with the possibilities; he would have his revenge on these nesters one way or the other, if they took his girl he would get his own back.

Bob was formulating a plan, when, to his surprise, Jennie turned off the trail about two miles out of Wainwright. She was heading for the Circle C!

Bob turned over the possibilities in his mind. Jennie Langton could be taking a message from her husband to Mart Simpson or merely paying a visit to a sick man. Whatever the reason it didn't matter to Bob, he could still fulfil his desires. Now he knew which route Jennie would take from the Circle C to the nesters' encampment it would be easier.

Jennie kept to a steady pace unaware of the cowboy who matched his speed to hers. A short time later Bob pulled to a halt at the top of a rise and watched Jennie ride up to the Circle C. She did not go inside the house but took a chair beside someone who was already on the verandah. Bob could not make out who it was but guessed it must be Mart Simpson when he recognized Joan Hedley, who joined them ten minutes later.

Jennie stayed another half hour before leaving the Circle C. Bob watched her for a few moments, then, satisfied about the route she was taking, set his horse across country. He kept the animal at a gallop until he reached the trail which Jennie would be following. About a quarter of a mile farther on it dipped through a narrow gully in the hillside as it dropped towards Sundance Hollow. Half-way along the gully was a clump of trees and, after hiding his horse, Bob made his way to the trees and quickly examined those overhanging the trail. When he had found what he was looking for he climbed the tree until he reached a branch which hung down over the trail. He tested its flexibility and, satisfied that it suited his purpose, he settled down to wait.

Bob stiffened when he heard the sound of horse's hooves. He fastened his neckerchief round his face making sure that it was secure no matter what happened.

The sound of the horse grew louder, and excitement gripped Bob when Jennie appeared riding steadily along the trail. He tensed himself, his hand placed carefully on the branch which he had tested. He watched Jennie intensely and then, judging the moment precisely, he pushed hard on the branch. It swung down and Jennie had no chance to avoid it. Her hands came up instinctively to protect herself as she swept straight into the branch. With nothing to hold on to she was knocked from the saddle with the impact. Before she had time to recover Bob dropped from the tree and was upon her gripping her wrists with one hand and forcing the other hard against her mouth. Everything had happened so quickly that in her dazed state, Jennie could grasp little of what was happening but the instinct to struggle was there. She twisted and turned but she was held in a grip that hurt. Suddenly she found the hold on her mouth gone but, before she could scream the hand swept viciously across her face, her head reeled, but through the haze she sensed a hand feeling for her body. She struggled harder but her attacker hit her hard again. Pain throbbed through her head; her senses were leaving her. Whatever happened she must stay conscious. She heard the tear as her blouse was ripped and felt a hand grasping at her skirt. Jennie renewed her efforts to escape but it was to no avail. She twisted and turned but then as she swung her head to one side it came up hard against a sharp stone. Vicious pain stabbed through her head. Her senses, already dazed, were flowing out of her, but just before she lost consciousness she felt the weight and power of the body above her suddenly relax and disappear completely.

The sound of an approaching horse penetrated Bob's excited mind as he felt resistance going out of Jennie. He listened again. There was no mistaking it. He cursed his luck that someone should ride this little used trail at this very time. He must not be seen. In a flash he was racing for his horse and a few moments later was riding away in the direction opposite to the approaching rider. After rounding a bend, and before he reached Sundance Hollow, Bob turned his horse up the hillside and once he reached the top sent the animal towards a section of Circle C ranch on which he knew that Charlie Raven and Grant Wells were working.

★ ★ ★

When Jamie reached the nesters' camp after leaving his sister in Wainwright the nesters gathered round for news of Mike.

"He's fine," reported Jamie. "And he's agreed to our plan. Jennie said he took a bit of persuading as he didn't want you to run any risks or get on the wrong side of the law."

"Mike needn't worry," said Ben. "We'll have to be all set to leave in a hurry when we get back. We are fairly well packed so if you womenfolk can have as much of the rest ready as soon as possible we'll be on the move immediately we return with Mike." He turned to Pete Nicholson and his wife. "If you don't want to be in on this, we understand, after all you owe us nothing."

Pete glanced at Myra and read her decision in her eyes. "We're with you," said Pete. "You were kind to us when Hedley turned us off our land. We'd like to stick with you."

"Fine," grinned Ben. "Pleased to have you."

"Where's Jennie?" asked Bess King.

"She must be here when you return."

"She will be," said Jamie. "She went to the Circle C to tell Mart what was happening and to arrange a meeting place if he is not fit to come today."

"Good," said Ben. "Jamie you'd better ride to meet Jennie. Don't worry we'll take care of Mike," he added quickly when Jamie started to protest. "Jennie had better know as soon as possible that we've left for Wainwright."

The nesters made their plans and when Jamie left to meet Jennie, Ben, Will, Tom and Pete rode in the direction of Wainwright.

★ ★ ★

Hank Barton, still feeling bruised and sore, insisted on taking a ride. He wanted to be in the saddle, out in the open and, seeing his determination, his mother let him go, warning him not to get into trouble again. At first he headed towards the section of the range being worked by his father and the Running W men but then changed his mind. Knowing that Mike Langton had been arrested and that the other nesters had been warned to be ready to move, he thought he would take a look at their encampment from a distance to see if they had taken heed of that warning.

Accordingly Hank cut across the grassland and turned into the gully leading into Sundance Hollow. He slowed his pace but checked it altogether when he saw a body lying beneath the trees a short distance ahead. He sat still on his horse, his eyes watching for any movement but there was none. His eyes searched the gully carefully but there was no sign of anyone else. Cautiously he sent his horse forward, his hand near his Colt. Suddenly his caution went when he saw that the body was that of a woman. He covered the remaining distance quickly, was soon out of the saddle and on his knees. Recognizing Jennie he was startled by the fact that her clothing was torn and ripped and blood oozed from a gash in the head.

Hank's thoughts raced with the possibilities of what had happened. There was no mistaking the fact that Jennie had been attacked, but by whom? He had neither seen nor heard anyone. He looked round desperately. His instinct was to go, to leave her, not to get involved, but in the act of straightening he stopped. Another trickle of blood dropped from the white forehead. He couldn't leave her; it might be a long time before anyone else rode this way. She could die. He must get her back to the nesters' camp. Hank dropped back on to his knees and bent over Jennie.

★ ★ ★

Jamie rode steadily along Sundance Hollow towards the gully which brought the trail into the hollow and which he knew his sister would take. She should be on her way back from the Circle C now. He was annoyed that he was not accompanying the men to Wainwright but he saw that it was sensible to let Jennie know that four determined men rode on a grim errand to Wainwright.

Jamie turned his horse into the gully and started the steady climb. Four hundred yards farther on he pulled his horse sharply to a halt. Jennie's horse was drinking from a small stream but there was no Jennie. Near panic seized Jamie. Where was she? What had happened to her? He stepped from the saddle and moved forward to the horse which looked up at his approach. Jamie's quiet voice soothed it and he gathered up the reins. He looked round anxiously. Jennie must have entered the gully but where was she now? Had she had an accident and fallen from the horse?

Jamie remounted and leading Jennie's horse he moved steadily up the gully, his eyes searching for any sign of his sister. He rode slowly round a turn but suddenly checked his horse. A man was bending over a figure on the ground. Jennie! Attacked!

Jamie slid quickly out of the saddle and secured the animals. Drawing his Colt he moved swiftly forward using every available piece of cover. The man straightened but he still had his back to Jamie. Then he dropped to his knees again and seemed to be handling Jennie's blouse.

"Hold it!" Jamie yelled, as he jumped from his cover a few yards away.

The man spun round. His eyes widened with shock and the fear of what discovery might bring.

"You!" gasped Jamie, recognizing Hank. Anger seethed in Jamie. Firing wagons was one thing but assaulting a woman was another, especially when it was his sister. Jamie's mind pounded, his trigger finger itched. It would be easy to pull the trigger, to drive death into this cattleman who had sought revenge on a nester's wife.

"I found her lyin' here — " started Hank.

"Don't try making excuses," snapped Jamie. "I know what I saw."

"But — "

"Shut up! Just unfasten that gun-belt."

Hank, his mind racing at the predicament he was in did as he was told.

"All right, git your horse over here." Jamie watched Hank carefully as he brought the animal nearer. "Git my sister on to it."

A few minutes later Jennie was slung across Hank's horse.

"Now, slowly and carefully down the gully," ordered Jamie.

Hank, covered by Jamie's gun, led the horse and when they reached the other two horses Jamie carefully kept Hank covered while they mounted.

The women in the camp hurried to meet the three horses when they saw them nearing the camp and recognized Jennie's figure slung across one of them. Their faces showed their concern, fearing the worst but hoping that things weren't as bad as they looked.

"What's happened?" asked Bess King, voicing the question which sprung to all their lips. There was no mistaking their surprise at seeing Hank Barton again. This time at the point of Jamie's gun.

"I found Hank Barton and Jennie; he'd attacked her and — "

"I didn't. I've tried to tell you what happened," protested Hank.

"Don't listen to him Jamie; it'll be a pack of lies," said Ethel Price sharply.

"I'm not," replied Jamie. "Take care of Jennie while I deal with this skunk."

The women were already taking the unconscious Jennie from the horse. Jamie indicated to Hank to dismount. When he had done so Jamie escorted him to the wagon and forced him to sit down with his back to one of the wheels.

"Bess, Bess, come over here," called Jamie when he saw that the women had got Jennie from the horse. When Bess came to him Jamie handed her his Colt. "Keep him covered while I tie him," he said.

A few minutes later Hank was securely tied and with Jennie tidied up and made as comfortable as possible the nesters settled down to an anxious wait wondering how things were going in Wainwright.

★ ★ ★

As they rode to town the nesters formulated a plan to rescue Mike. They discussed several alternatives but finally settled for the simplest and most straightforward.

The result was that just before they reached Wainwright Will King took the spare horse and, accompanied by Pete Nicholson, entered the town from a different direction. They made their way carefully through the back streets and alleys until they were behind the jail.

As Will and Pete had the longer ride, Ben Price and Tom Byron timed their ride carefully so that they came to the narrow street behind the jail for only a moment to check that Will and Pete were in position. Satisfied, they turned into the main street and rode to the sheriff's office. The afternoon was hot and only two people stirred on the sidewalk beyond the sheriff's office. A few horses were outside the saloon, flicking their tails against the pestering flies, while their riders were inside the saloon slaking their thirst against the heat of the day.

The two nesters pulled up outside the sheriff's office, slipped from the saddles and strolled into the building. Sheriff Lever, dozing in his chair, his feet propped on his desk, was totally unprepared to see two Colts suddenly appear in the hands of the nesters.

"Take it quietly, sheriff," said Ben, "and no one will get hurt."

"You can't — " started the wide-eyed lawman.

"We can and will," cut in Tom. "On your feet." He moved swiftly behind the sheriff and as he stood up Tom whipped his gun hard across the lawman's head. Instantly Ben holstered his gun and grabbed a bunch of keys from the hook close to the door leading to the cells. A moment later he was releasing an excited and eager Mike.

Tom appeared dragging the sheriff after him and, after disarming him, the nesters soon had him tied, gagged and locked in his cell. Mike left by the back door and he, together with Will and Pete, rode quickly through the back streets while Ben and Tom casually left by the front door, mounted their horses and rode slowly out of Wainwright.

Two miles from Wainwright they met up with their three friends.

"Simple," said Ben with a broad smile. "Mike won't be missed until the sheriff's found. Let's ride."

The five men put their horses into a gallop, anxious to gain as much lead as possible on the posse which must inevitably follow.

Reaching the edge of the hill above

Sundance Hollow they did not hesitate but thundered down the hillside towards the camp.

The pound of the hooves and the sight of the horsemen brought Jamie and the womenfolk to their feet. Jamie's eyes took in the five men and he let out a whoop.

"They made it! They've got Mike!" He turned with a broad grin to see everyone smiling with delight, while Nicholson's two young sons jumped up and down with excitement.

The riders rode into camp fast bringing their mounts to a dust-stirring halt, but their smiles vanished when they saw Jennie's silent form and Hank Barton tied to the wagon wheel.

"What's happened?" yelled Mike. He jumped from the saddle before his horse had stopped and raced to his wife.

Jamie was beside him quickly explaining what had happened. Mike's brain whirled as the story unfolded. He straightened from the silent figure and turned towards Hank Barton. He stared hard at him, anger, hate and detestation pouring from him yet hardly able to believe this eighteen-year-old had been capable of this assault. Mike could have understood it better if it had been Bob Barton after the way he had handled Jennie on that first meeting in Sioux Hollow.

Mike's instinct was to beat Barton to death, and, for one moment the anxious Jamie thought that Mike was going to do just that but then he saw some of the tension leave Mike, and he saw a worried look cross his face as if he was battling with a difficult problem.

Suddenly he turned to the others. "Ben, Will, Tom, I'm grateful for what you've done but I can't go!" He glanced round everyone. "I don't want to hold you back. You have committed a crime breaking me out of jail. We figured the posse wouldn't bother with us once it became obvious we were leaving; I reckon they still won't especially if I'm here."

"We can all go," urged Will. "Jennie will be all right in the wagon."

"No," said Mike. "From what you tell me Jennie's been unconscious for longer than I like. She must have the doctor."

"I'll fetch him," said Jamie, anxious to do something for his sister.

"Wait," said Mike. "The sheriff will have been found by now, a nester wouldn't have a chance of getting near the doc, but I figure I can make it safe to do so."

The others looked puzzled. "What do you mean?" asked Will.

"I'll take young Barton to his pa, tell him what's happened, and tell him to drop the charge against me or I'll talk. If I do that Hank will have to stand trial and that will be one charge Barton won't be able to squash even with all his influence. Jamie if you'll ride with me I figure Barton will make Wainwright safe enough to fetch the doc to Jennie."

"I figure if you stop we all stop," said Ben.

"I don't want you to run any more risks on my account," said Mike.

Ben looked at the others who voiced their approval of his suggestion.

"Thanks," said Mike with a grateful smile. "Right, let's get young Barton to his father before the sheriff and his posse arrive."

A horse was got ready for Hank Barton and then after he was forced to mount the horse and his hands were tied behind his back, the party of seven riders headed out of Sundance Hollow for the Running W.

They rode silently, each lost in his own thoughts but alert to the possible appearance of a posse from the direction of Wainwright but none came and as the miles went by confidence grew in the nesters that the posse would not appear and that they would be able to confront Al Barton alone.

That hope was shattered when they topped the rise and saw ten horsemen riding fast up the slope towards them. Mike halted his party and waited, eyeing the approaching riders carefully.

"Al Barton's there," he observed. Will and Ben moved closer to Hank, killing any thought he had of escape.

"The sheriff's there," said Jamie, glancing anxiously at Mike.

Mike cursed; so where nesters were concerned the sheriff was very much under the influence of Al Barton. Mike had wanted this between Al Barton and himself, now it would have to come out in front of others. His bargaining position was weakened. He would have to explain Hank's presence as a prisoner and that would leave him no room to strike a price for his silence. But there was nothing to be done now, he would have to play it as it came.

The sheriff and the posse kept to their fast pace even though they saw the riders at the top of the slope and were surprised when they recognized them as the men they were hunting. It puzzled Al. Why were they riding this way? His eyes swept across them and the shock he received almost caused him to rein in his horse. The nesters had Hank. How? Why? The questions thundered in Al's mind but he had no answer.

Hands strayed nearer Colts but the nesters kept theirs well away from their weapons letting the cattlemen see that they did not mean to fight.

"What you doing with my son?" boomed Al, taking the leadership out of the hands of the sheriff. Al steadied his horse as he demanded information.

"We bring him back to his father to be punished," called Mike.

"Punished? What's he done?"

"He attacked my wife. She is back in our camp still unconscious."

"What!" Al was incredulous. "I don't believe it."

"He was seen."

"By one of your nesters, I suppose," snapped Al contemptuously.

Before Mike could speak, Jamie stabbed his horse a couple of paces forward. "I saw him." His voice was soft but precise, definite in its statement. Jamie went on quickly telling what he had seen.

Al listened without speaking, his face darkening as the story proceeded.

"Is this true?" he shouted to Hank, when Jamie had finished.

"No, pa, it's not," called Hank. "I found her lying unconscious her clothes all torn."

"I don't believe him," shouted Mike. "We would have dealt with him but I thought you cattlemen had a reputation for respecting women. If that is so you'll deal with him." Mike turned to Ben. "Release him."

Ben did not question the decision but did as he was told.

As soon as he felt his hands freed, Hank sent his horse forward to join his father. Al was puzzled by Mike's action but he realized it placed him in an awkward position.

"We don't let the matter stop there Langton," called Al. "I don't think my son — " The words faltered. A dull roar came faintly to the ears of the group, a sound a cattleman did not like to hear. "But there must be a mistake. Hank wouldn't — " The sound was there again, a little louder and this time there was no mistaking it.

All eyes turned in its direction. The first tremor of hundreds of thundering hooves made themselves felt and a dust cloud rose across the grassland.

"Stampede!" yelled Al.

"From the Circle C!" shouted the sheriff.

For a moment the whole group were frozen by the horror, realizing the death and carnage which could follow the pounding, tearing hooves.

The steers were far across the grassland but in a moment it was apparent that their run would take them over the edge and down into Sundance Hollow.

"Jennie!" yelled Mike and in the same moment stabbed his horse forward, but already one rider had broken from the group and his horse was in full gallop.

9

HANK BARTON was the first to realize that the stampede was heading for Sundance Hollow and that if it could not be turned before then it would over-run the nesters' camp. And there lay an unconscious woman Jennie, the only person who might be able to prove his innocence!

He stabbed his horse hard and shot away from the group before anyone realized what was happening. The animal stretched itself into a full gallop and earth flew as it tore across the grassland. He was thankful that the nesters had put him on a strong but supple animal which responded to his bidding. He turned the horse, judging the angle with the herd so that he could reach the leading steers before they plunged into Sundance Hollow. A glance over his shoulder told him that the cattlemen and nesters alike were in full cry behind him all bent on the same purpose, to stop the stampede and prevent the cattle from over-running the nesters' camp.

The thunder of the stampeding hooves grew louder as the riders kept their horses to a rescue-bent gallop. Horsemen desperately tried to get more from their mounts which stretched themselves to the full as they attempted to answer the urgent calls.

The angle narrowed. Hank watched the steers carefully. There was still some distance to go before he could make contact with the stampeding herd which raced onward. The lead steers must be turned before they reached the edge of the slope into Sundance Hollow. The next five minutes seemed like an eternity to Hank. It took him nearer the herd but he had gained nothing on the leaders. He ventured a glance over his shoulder. Riders were strung out across the grassland with his father and Mike Langton nearest to him. Their attention was concentrated on the stampeding cattle. They were determined on turning the herd. Hank looked beyond the lead steers to the edge of Sundance Hollow. There was still some way to go but it would be touch and go as to whether they would be able to turn the cattle in time.

Suddenly Hank turned his horse away, checking it slightly. His father and Mike thundered past, and Hank caught a glimpse of the startled look on his father's face.

In spite of the desperate situation and the concentrated effort of the fast ride and determination to succeed, Al still had time to admire his younger son's efforts. He had been the first to realize the situation, he had been first away and rode with a determination as if he was bent on turning the stampede himself. It shocked Al when he saw his son check his horse and turn away. Hank had pulled out; scared when it mattered most. Al almost checked his horse but there was a more desperate need right now and Al urged his horse onwards. He was neck and neck with Mike and when he saw the anxious look on the nester's face, he realized the anguish he must be feeling. If the cattle weren't stopped his wife would be doomed.

They were close to the steers. The roar of the thundering hooves seemed to fill the Montana sky. Desperate men called to their horses for more effort but they gained little on the leaders. Then suddenly it was too late. They could never reach the lead steers and turn them in time. But still the men rode, desperate and anxious, hoping for some miracle to happen.

The edge of the slope came nearer and nearer Mike yelled at his horse for one last desperate effort. For one moment he seemed to gain and then the hooves pounded over the edge and down the slope into Sundance Hollow!

After turning his horse Hank put the

animal into full stride. He shouted, cajoled and threatened and the powerful horse seemed to find extra strength to flay the earth quicker with its pounding hooves. Hank sent the horse towards Sundance Hollow. He glanced across the grassland and estimated he would hit the edge of Sundance Hollow nearly a mile to the west of the stampeding herd.

Hank was tense as he drove his mount desperately on. There was just a chance he might succeed, but it would be touch and go. He reached the slope before the herd and put his horse unhesitatingly straight over the edge and kept it to a fast gallop down the incline. He had judged the position nicely and found himself heading straight for the nesters' camp.

The women were already on their feet staring with frightened looks at the hillside, unaware of what was causing the thundering sound which flowed out over the hill and flooded down into the hollow around them. Then they saw the lone horseman and read a warning of impending disaster in the fast, urgent ride.

"Hank Barton!" gasped Bess, in surprise. "What's happened?"

"What's the noise?" asked a frightened Ethel, as if seeking some reassuring explanation.

"Look!" Myra Nicholson's eyes widened with intense fear as she pointed to the hillside, and then she clutched her two sons, Billy and Dan, close to her.

The women gazed at the hillside and saw steers plunging over the edge and thundering down the slope. Dust rose, the earth trembled as steer after steer poured over the ridge. The nesters stood petrified, unable to believe what they were seeing. They were frozen to the spot as if fixed by the sight of the stampeding herd, its mass of heaving flesh plunging downwards.

Then Hank was among them pulling his mount to an earth-tearing halt. He was out of the saddle almost before it had stopped. He glanced back at the herd plunging at an ever increasing pace into Sundance Hollow. Riders were close to the herd trying desperately to turn it along the hollow away from the camp but one glance was sufficient to tell him that they were not in the right position to do so. Some men were close to the leaders but wrongly placed to turn them. The steers were filling the hollow as they raced onwards. The nesters' camp was doomed!

"Quick", yelled Hank. "To the river."

The women turned quickly. Myra grasped her sons' hands and raced for the water. Martha Byron and Bess King grasped at some belongings but Hank grabbed them and propelled them towards the water.

"Get going," he yelled. "You haven't time for anything else!"

"Jennie!" screamed Ethel. "What about Jennie?"

"I'll get her," yelled Hank.

Four strides took him to the unconscious form and he swept her up into his arms. Steers were pounding nearer and nearer. Horsemen desperately tried to halt the stampede. Hank ran for the river.

"Into the water everybody," he shouted. "As far as you can."

Myra picked up Billy and Bess grabbed Dan as they entered the gently flowing water and waded up to their waists.

"Can you two take Mrs Langton?" shouted Hank.

Martha and Ethel nodded and, after moving away from the river bank, took the unconscious form from Hank.

He pushed his thighs against the water. It seemed eternity before they were free of its drag. All the time he had been anxiously watching the oncoming cattle. The thunder of their hooves was frightening, but his horse was still near the wagon. If he could reach it before it scared he would be in front of the herd, in a good position to try to turn the lead steers. Riders were closing in on the flanks and one rider was pulling slightly ahead. Hank raced towards his horse but suddenly the animal, frightened by the thunder in the valley, bolted. Hank pulled up sharp. His chance of helping the rider who had got ahead of the cattle had gone. He turned and saw the steers with flying hooves pounding down upon him. The river was his only chance. His feet beat the earth in his attempt to reach the safety of the water. He might just make it. His foot stubbed the ground; he stumbled and could not save himself. He hit the earth driving the breath from his body. The desperateness of his predicament brought him scrambling to his feet but he realized it was now too late. He would never reach the river.

* * *

Mike Langton's mind was in a panic as the stampeding cattle raced to the edge of Sundance Hollow. He had figured that because of the angle at which they would hit the slope they would naturally swing to the right once they reached the bottom and that meant straight through the nesters' camp and he had left Jennie there unconscious! They must turn those steers!

Mike drove his horse harder and the animal, sensing the urgency, found hidden strength. They gained on the lead steers. Mike was oblivious to the other riders but he knew that they would be doing their utmost to stop this stampede which could spell destruction to everything in its path as well as to valuable steers should any lose their footing.

Suddenly Mike realized they could never stop the herd before it reached Sundance Hollow. He was horrified; he was lost. What do they do now? He cursed his lack of experience with herds as big as this. There was a rider alongside him. A glance showed him the worried but determined look on Al Barton's face. He saw concern there and realized that it was concern for the people who lay in the path of the stampede. Al yelled and pointed. At the same time Al turned his horse to take the slope at a different angle to the cattle. Mike followed suit and, as they plunged over the edge at full gallop, realized the wisdom of Al's change of direction. The different angle of approach put them closer to the lead steers by the time the cattle reached the bottom of the slope and turned along Sundance Hollow.

Racing beside the cattle, Al indicated that they must put pressure on the leaders, try to turn them in upon themselves, pressurize them from this side and the herd would swing towards the river. The two men urged their horses faster. They were alongside the lead steers. Then Mike saw the encampment. They would never stop the cattle in time. It seemed eternity to Mike before his horse got ahead of the stampede. Mike yelled to the animal. The cattle couldn't be turned in time, so could he outpace them and save Jennie? Desperate anxiety caused him to lash the horse. Then he saw figures running to the river, and behind them someone picked something up and started running towards the water. Someone was saving Jennie! Mike's brain pounded with relief. But who was it? No man had been left behind.

Mike pulled a few more yards ahead. A glance over his shoulder told him that Al was beginning to draw ahead of the stampede. Mike decided to wait before he did anything. Jennie was safe and now he could follow Al Barton's actions to do what he could to help bring the herd under control.

Mike started. The man who had rescued Jennie was leaving the safety of the river and was racing towards his horse. Suddenly the horse bolted and the man turned. Mike gasped. Hank Barton! Hank Barton had rescued Jennie! He hadn't been escaping as Mike had assumed. When others had automatically thought of turning the herd to save the nesters Hank had thought of warning the nesters, giving them a chance if the herd couldn't be turned. And this was a youngster who had shown no love for nesters, yet he had saved the woman he had assaulted. It didn't make sense. If he had not warned the nesters and the herd had overrun the encampment, Jennie would die and the person who could utter his final condemnation would be dead. Unless — The thoughts were through Mike's head in a flash. Unless Hank was innocent and Jennie could prove it!

Hank was running for the river. Mike edged his horse farther across the front of the herd. Mike yelled, shocked by the sight of Hank's fall. He turned his horse, still at full gallop, towards the figure on the ground.

Hank scrambled to his feet. He was dazed by the predicament and felt the grip of icy fear as the herd thundered dawn upon him. He started to turn, to run instinctively, then there was a horse bearing down on him fast. The rider was yelling. Everything came sharply to Hank. He saw rescue and braced himself. As the rider checked his horse he leaned down and extended his right arm. Hank grasped it and, springing upwards, was helped by the rider's pull. He swung up behind the horseman who in the same instant sent his mount racing ahead of the herd. For a few moments the leading steers gained. The extra weight on the horse's back was telling. The thundering hooves pounded the earth behind the horse and its riders. Then the animal found its stride and held its own. With extra efforts it widened the gap and when Mike judged it to be right he edged the horse nearer and nearer the river. Then they were close to the water and Mike with a sudden turn sent the animal into the river. The pace took the horse deep and the impact sent both men tumbling into the water and the stampeding cattle thundered past.

★ ★ ★

Al Barton had seen his son running for his horse and instinctively willed his horse faster but knew he was in no position to help. He cried out for his boy to move faster. He saw the horse bolt, his son turn and fall. Al turned his horse to help but, realizing he was too near the lead steers to ever get across them and reach Hank, he checked the horse and galloped with the herd. Anxiety and fear were in his eyes when he saw Mike turn towards Hank and tension mounted until he saw the horse with the two riders plunge into the water. His mind pounded as he turned his concentration back to outriding and slowing the herd. Langton had saved his son. Saved Hank who stood accused of assaulting Langton's wife. He could have sought his revenge by leaving Hank to the tearing, death-dealing hooves of the scared steers. But he hadn't. He'd risked his own life to save Hank!

Al's horse had taken him ahead of the running cattle and when he glanced round to size up the situation he saw that several riders were alongside the front of the herd. As one of his cowboys pulled ahead he cut across the front of the herd and he and Al weaved backwards and forwards attempting to slow the cattle down. At the same time the cowboys on the right flank gradually increased their pressure on the leaders forcing them closer together and, as the river swung away from them, trying to turn them into a circle.

They covered another five miles before they were successful and during that time Al saw the nesters, whom he figured would have had only a little experience of cattle and probably none at all of a stampede, throw themselves wholeheartedly into the task of stopping the cattle even though they had seen their belongings and wagons shattered as the herd swept through the encampment. The nesters, following the cowboys' lead, quickly adapted themselves to what was required and the cattlemen had to admire their horsemanship and adaptability.

Once the herd was milling in a huge controlled mass Sheriff Lever sought out Al.

"Figure I'd better get Langton," he called.

"I'll be with you," said Al as he wiped the dust and sweat from his red face and eased himself in his saddle. "Saw him save Hank."

"What!" The sheriff showed his surprise.

As they rode Al related what he had seen. "Might just drop the charge after that," he added when he had finished his story.

"And what about the assault charge which might have to be brought against Hank?" queried the sheriff.

"I still don't believe he did it."

"From what Langton said things looked stacked against Hank."

Half-way back to what had been the nesters' camp a group of riders approached them at the gallop.

"Circle C, a bit late," observed Al with a grin.

Zeke Hedley slowed his riders and brought them to a halt when he saw Al Barton and the sheriff.

"Thanks for what you've done, Al," he called. "Sure was lucky you were out on that part of the range."

"Thank the nesters too," replied Al. "It would have taken a bit longer and you'd have lost more cattle if it hadn't been for their help."

"Sure will," said Zeke. "Heard a bit about it from Langton back there. Surprised to see him. Hear he broke jail. What happens now?"

"Just on our way to sort it out," said the sheriff.

Zeke nodded. He would have said more but he didn't want to interfere any more than necessary. "Wal, we'll get the cattle and relieve your men. Thanks again Al."

"How did it happen?" queried Al.

"Don't know. We were workin' another part of the range. It was the noise that drew our attention but we were too far away to do anything. Somethin' must have spooked them."

"Lose many?" asked Al as they started to move away.

"A few."

"Reckon they'll be a bit thinner after that run."

"Soon fatten 'em up again," replied Zeke and sent his horse in the direction of his cattle.

Al and the sheriff rode on to find the nesters' womenfolk trying to find something in the ruins of their belongings but there was little which was of any use after the heaving bodies and tearing hooves had thundered through their camp.

The nesters stopped their search at the approach of the horsemen. They watched them apprehensively, wondering what their attitude would be. Al stopped his horse and swung from the saddle. The sheriff followed but left the play to Al.

The cattleman looked hard at Hank

and smiled then stepped towards Mike who supported Jennie, his arm around her waist as she clung to him as if wanting to hold him back from some catastrophe.

Mike faced the new arrivals grimly. With the sheriff accompanying Al Barton it could only mean one thing — arrest. If he was arrested every man who broke him out of jail would have to be arrested too, and with their belongings ruined by the stampede the outcome was inevitable — the end of their stay in this part of Montana, if not in the whole of Montana, for the name would have too many unhappy memories.

Al stared hard at Mike for a moment then suddenly extended his hand. "Thanks for saving my son's life," he said. There was no mistaking his depth of gratitude.

Seconds paused before Mike seemed to realize what Al had said and that he was offering him his hand. Then he took it and felt a warm grip.

"Hank saved my wife, I'm more than grateful."

Al was startled. "Saved your wife?" he said.

"I thought you must know," said Mike.

"I saw you save Hank," replied Al. "I wondered what he was doing there in front of the stampede."

"While everyone else thought the only way was to turn the herd, Hank thought of the women left in the camp. He was the only one who realized they were doomed if we failed to turn the cattle and as it happened he was right and I'll be forever in his debt."

"I never saw anything of that. It seems we are both indebted to each other. I'm willing to forget everything if you are."

"You mean there'll be no more pushing us on? We can stay?"

Al nodded. "Sure."

Mike smiled and looked round to the womenfolk. There was relief in their eyes, their husbands would not be charged with the jail-break but he knew there was still tension, still a fear.

Mike looked back at Al. "They're worried; are the men all right?"

"Yes," replied Al. "They did a great job, no one was hurt; they should be back before long. You all saw the Circle C, well they'll be takin' over." The tension eased in the nesters and Al turned his attention back to Mike and Jennie. "What about Mrs Langton? I hope you are recovered."

"Just about," replied Jennie, though it was obvious that she was still shaken.

"Jennie will be all right," said Mike. "She's still a bit dazed. Apparently she came round just after Hank had saved her. I've been asking her about the attack but she is still a bit hazy about it."

"Was it Hank, Mrs Langton?" asked Al, concern showing on his face. "I must know," he added as Jennie hesitated. "Don't keep the truth from me even though Hank saved your life."

Jennie frowned. "I don't really know," she replied despairingly, wanting to be able to answer truthfully, wanting to be able to identify her attacker.

The sheriff stepped forward. "Mrs Langton," he said gently, "Maybe if we went over what happened you might remember something."

Mike started to protest that Jennie wasn't up to recalling the experience again but Jennie stopped him.

"I'd rather try," she said. "Hank says he didn't attack me, so I'd like to try to clear things up."

"Good," said the sheriff. "Now if you like to tell us what happened, take your time and try to remember everything no matter how trivial, it may help identify the man who attacked you."

Jennie started her story from the time she left the Circle C but when she reached the point where she was knocked from her horse the sheriff stopped her.

"This person must have known you

were riding that way, he was waiting for you, now, did you see anyone following you?"

"No."

"Did anyone know you were going to the Circle C?"

"Only Mike and Jamie."

"Who was at the Circle C?"

"Only Joan and Mart."

"You didn't see anyone else?"

"No."

"Could someone have followed you from town or even seen you on your way to the Circle C and followed you?"

"I suppose so."

"Could it have been Hank?" The sheriff directed his question at Al.

"Yes," replied Al firmly. "He'd left the Running W; I suppose he could have seen Mrs Langton and followed her."

"I didn't pa, I didn't," Hank shouted. He turned to Jennie. "Tell them it wasn't me, tell them."

A look of despair crossed Jennie's

face and she felt Mike's comforting arm go round her shoulder.

"Try to remember, Jennie, anything, anything at all," he said.

"All right, Mrs Langton, please carry on," said the sheriff. "The branch of the tree knocked you from your horse."

"Yes and someone dropped out of the tree and was on top of me before I could get up."

"Was there anything about him you can remember?"

Jennie shook her head. "No. His neckerchief was pulled up over his face. He pressed his hand hard across my mouth and — " Her voice trailed away. Something flashed into her mind; something she had remembered, but could she be certain?

The men sensed that her hesitancy meant something of significance. They looked at her expectantly, seeing the change on her face showing that she might have thought of something.

"What is it Jennie?" prompted Mike.

Jennie's brain was racing, going over

that moment time and time again, trying to see it more vividly, trying to see more clearly the one thing which had struck her. Then suddenly it was there, sharp, significant. She stared at Al and then at Hank.

"Oh, no it wasn't Hank," she whispered slowly.

The men stared at her waiting for more.

"How can you be sure?" asked the sheriff.

"It wasn't Hank," she repeated as she stared vacantly before her, her thoughts far away.

"Jennie, how do you know?" asked Mike.

Suddenly Jennie started. She was back with them. She looked from one to the other. She saw relief on the faces of Al and his son. But still there was curiosity there, a desire to know.

"The man who attacked me wore a ring. I felt it. I saw it. Hank doesn't wear a ring!"

"What kind of ring?" asked the sheriff.

"Please try to remember anything about it. It might help to identify him."

"Can you remember?" put in Mike.

A curious look came into Jennie's eyes. "Oh, I do remember, I can see it vividly." She paused, thinking and seeing a ring on the man who attacked her and recalling that she had seen it before on a man who had handled her on her first day in Sioux Hollow when she watched Mike tortured. No one spoke, each waiting expectantly. "It was a broad gold ring," said Jennie softly and slowly, "and engraved on it was a buffalo's head!"

Jennie saw the pain and hurt come across Al's face and she felt sorry for him. Deep down all along he had known Hank to be innocent just as now deep down he knew those words to be true. Hank started, a look of disbelief in his eyes. His gaze passed from Jennie to his father.

"Pa, that's Bob's ring!" he whispered incredulously.

"I know, son, I know."

10

AL BARTON'S turmoiled thoughts were interrupted by the sound of hoof-beats. He turned to see smiling nesters riding in and watched them reunited with their wives and friends and joyously receive the news that they could stay, that there would be no more hounding by Al Barton. He saw them check their desire to come and thank him as they received the news about Bob.

With a sad heart he turned towards his horse but Mike stopped him. "Is there anything we can do?" he asked.

"Thanks, Langton," he said. "I don't think there is. This is a job for the sheriff and myself. Come on we'd better find Bob."

He swung into the saddle and waited for the sheriff to mount up.

"Hold it, pa. I'm ridin' with you,"

Hank shouted and turned to Mike. "Can I borrow a horse, Mr Langton?"

"Sure, Hank," replied Mike.

Hank hurried to select a horse and was rejoining his father and the sheriff when the sound of hard ridden horses, approaching from the direction of the herd, took everybody's attention wondering who was in such a hurry and why.

A few moments later they recognized Zeke Hedley and his daughter accompanied by Mart Simpson. Everyone was surprised and delighted to see him in the saddle but these feelings were overshadowed by the obvious signs which spelt trouble.

As the three riders checked their horses, Mart exchanged greetings with his friends and reassured them he was all right, but Zeke turned to Al pulling up alongside him.

"Hoped I might catch you before you left," he said. There was concern and trouble showing on his face. "Al, I'm afraid I've some bad news for you."

"Not more," said Al. "It can't be worse than what I already know."

Zeke looked puzzled and Hank, realizing he didn't know to what his father was referring, offered an explanation. "Mrs Langton was attacked earlier today. We have just heard it was Bob."

"What!" Zeke gasped and exchanged glances with a startled Joan and Mart. He looked back at Al. "I'm sorry, Al, real sorry especially as what we have to tell you will only add to your troubles."

"Go on, then, get on with it," said Al as Zeke paused. "If there's worse don't hold it back. Let me have it all at once."

Zeke glanced at Joan who pushed her horse forward. "After Jennie visited Mart, I thought a short ride might do him good. The doctor had said he should start getting out more. Mart felt like trying it and, as he has been showing an interest in the Circle C, I thought he might like to see more of it. We headed to the north, the hills there give a better view. It was while we were out that we saw Bob in the distance, I recognized his sit on a horse. He seemed in a mighty hurry so, thinking something might be wrong, we followed. We saw him make contact with the two new men dad had signed on, Charlie Raven and Grant Wells. We were about to forget the whole thing thinking there had been nothing to Bob's fast ride but something personal when they rode off together in the direction of the herd which dad was running on the north range. We still did not suspect anything and turned for home but as it happened our route kept the herd in sight. We were astounded when the three of them started to move those cattle and even more astonished when we realized they were scaring the steers into a stampede!"

"What! Bob responsible for the stampede? What sort of a cattleman is he?" Al was both shocked and disgusted.

"I'm sorry, Mr Barton," went on

Joan. "Bob deliberately stampeded those cattle."

"Then from what we saw when we first sighted the stampede he purposely headed them for Sundance Hollow," said Al.

"It certainly looked like it from where we were," put in Mart.

Al looked thoughtful. "Bob assaulted Jennie, was disturbed by Hank and left her unconscious. He would surmise that the natural thing to do would be to take Jennie to this camp. He stampeded the cattle after assaulting Jennie and deliberately headed them for Sundance Hollow."

Zeke gasped. "You mean this was a deliberate attempt to kill Jennie in case she had identified him."

"Could be," muttered Al. "Why else stampede the cattle?"

"Destroy our camp, so make us want to move on," put in Mike.

"Sure, he would achieve two objectives, killed Jennie and made you decide to move."

"But why my cattle?" put in Zeke.

"Nearest to Sundance Hollow," explained Al. "But it also looks as if he had two accomplices planted on the Circle C."

Zeke let out a low whistle. "If that's so then he could have primed them to kill those two steers and plant them on Pete Nicholson."

Al nodded. "Seems more than likely now, after what has happened. I know he didn't like you fencin' Zeke, I know he hated nesters."

"It looks as if he went farther than tarring and feathering Mart to put the nesters and Circle C at each other," commented Joan.

"He did that too?" gasped Al.

"He was behind it, let it slip out one day when he was talking to me," said Joan.

Al's face darkened. "Come on Chris, let's find him. Seems my son was — "

"Won't be any need," said the sheriff and nodded in the direction of a horse rider who had broken the skyline and started down the slope towards the camp.

Al stiffened in the saddle. "A case of wanting to see if his crime's paid off," he muttered.

"Act as if we know nothing," warned the sheriff as everyone turned to stare at the rider in angry silence. "He must ride right in here suspecting nothing."

Although the tension was still there people started to talk to each other, but Al silently watched his son ride in.

"Howdy," grinned Bob as he joined the group. Suddenly his smile vanished when he saw Mike. "What's he doin' here? Thought he was in jail." Al, who had been watching Bob carefully, thought he detected a momentary look of shock when Bob saw Jennie.

"I was busted out by my friends," replied Mike.

"What!" Bob glanced sharply at the sheriff. "Then why aren't you arrestin' them? Or maybe you're lettin' them off seeing they won't be stayin'."

263

"What do you mean?" asked the sheriff.

"Heard about the stampede, looks as if it tore straight through the camp. Reckon if it was me I'd want to move on."

"Well, it ain't you," rapped Al, startling his son with the viciousness of his tone. "These nesters are stayin'. Those who want can move into Sioux Hollow. I'll not worry 'em, in fact I'll help them get started again. If I'm not mistaken Zeke will feel the same, especially after the way they helped me save his cattle."

"Sure, only too glad," agreed Zeke.

Bob stared at the two ranchers. "You two gone mad?" he shouted. "These are nesters, they'll take you and they'll — "

"You wearin' your ring?" boomed Al interrupting Bob's outburst.

"Sure, but — " Bob automatically held his hand up.

"Mrs Langton recognized it!" yelled Al. Before Bob realized what was happening his father stabbed his horse forward and sent him reeling from the saddle with a vicious blow across the face. He landed on his back, hitting the earth hard and astonishment showed on his face.

His father glowered down at him. "Bartons, like most cattlemen have always respected womenfolk. No son of mine assaults a woman and gets away with it!"

Anger crossed Bob's face. He cursed himself for his carelessness about the ring. Words of protestation sprang to his lips.

"Don't deny it," shouted Al with contempt, "and don't deny you deliberately started the stampede, Joan and Mart saw you! What did you want to do, kill Jennie in case she recognized you? Bust the nesters' camp and make them want to move on?"

Bob had scrambled to his feet. Hate poured from his eyes as he looked at his father. "Guess, go on keep on guessing."

"I will," lashed back Al. "You tried to set the Circle C and nesters at each others throats by tarring and feathering Mart, tried again by getting two side-kicks on the Circle C pay-roll to cause trouble like killing and planting two steers on Pete Nicholson. Thank goodness Zeke kept a large portion of self-control through it all."

"Zeke was soft and you were softening," stormed Bob, seemingly unaware that he was condemning himself. "Someone had to do something to get these nesters out. You and Zeke — "

"Take him, sheriff," cut in Al disgustedly.

Bob spun round to face the lawman like a cornered animal only to find himself staring into the cold muzzle of a Colt.

"All right, Bob, just take it easy," said the sheriff, his voice quiet but firm, his eyes alert for a suspicious move. He moved forward slowly, ignoring the hatred burning in Bob's eyes.

Bob stiffened as the lawman carefully removed his Colt from its holster. "Mount up Bob," he ordered.

After Bob was in the saddle the sheriff swung on to his horse keeping the young man under his vigilant eye all the time. Firmly seated in the saddle he indicated Bob to move.

Bob did not glance at his father as he turned his horse and rode slowly away from the camp followed by the sheriff.

Al watched them for a few minutes then as he turned in the saddle Mike stepped forward.

"I'd like to move back to Sioux Hollow, Mr Barton," he said.

"It's open country." A faint smile flicked his lips for a moment and then was gone.

"Think I'll make that move too," said Tom. "Will and Ben feel like staying here, neighbours to the Nicholsons."

"I figure there's one nester who'll be taking more interest in cattle from now on," grinned Zeke indicating Mart who exchanged a smile with Joan.

A shot rang out halting any more planning. Everyone stared in silence across the hollow. A lone horseman was heading their way. No one spoke a word as a grim-faced sheriff rode up.

He stopped his horse in front of Al. "I'm sorry, Al," he said quietly. "He tried to jump me. There was nothing I could do."

For a moment Al did not speak. He thought of the son he once knew and of the son he had become. "That's all right, Chris, you did what you had to do. Maybe it's for the best, maybe he can be spared the disgrace."

"Sure, Al. I'll fix things."

"Thanks. I've lost a son but," Al turned to Hank, "I've gained a man. Want to ride with me?"

"Sure pa." In spite of the tragedy Hank's face lit up. Now his pa accepted him as a man.

"Come on, then, I guess your ma is goin' to need us."

Other titles in the Linford Western Library:

TOP HAND
Wade Everett

The Broken T was big. But no ranch is big enough to let a man hide from himself.

GUN WOLVES OF LOBO BASIN
Lee Floren

The Feud was a blood debt. When Smoke Talbot found the outlaws who gunned down his folks he aimed to nail their hide to the barn door.

SHOTGUN SHARKEY
Marshall Grover

The westbound coach carrying the indomitable Larry and Stretch headed for a shooting showdown.

FIGHTING RAMROD
Charles N. Heckelmann

Most men would have cut their losses, but Frazer counted the bullets in his guns and said he'd soak the range in blood before he'd give up another inch of what was his.

LONE GUN
Eric Allen

Smoke Blackbird had been away too long. The Lequires had seized the Blackbird farm, forcing the Indians and settlers off, and no one seemed willing to fight! He had to fight alone.

THE THIRD RIDER
Barry Cord

Mel Rawlins wasn't going to let anything stand in his way. His father was murdered, his two brothers gone. Now Mel rode for vengeance.

ARIZONA DRIFTERS
W. C. Tuttle

When drifting Dutton and Lonnie Steelman decide to become partners they find that they have a common enemy in the formidable Thurston brothers.

TOMBSTONE
Matt Braun

Wells Fargo paid Luke Starbuck to outgun the silver-thieving stagecoach gang at Tombstone. Before long Luke can see the only thing bearing fruit in this eldorado will be the gallows tree.

HIGH BORDER RIDERS
Lee Floren

Buckshot McKee and Tortilla Joe cut the trail of a border tough who was running Mexican beef into Texas. They stopped the smuggler in his tracks.

BRETT RANDALL, GAMBLER
E. B. Mann

Larry Day had the choice of running away from the law or of assuming a dead man's place. No matter what he decided he was bound to end up dead.

THE GUNSHARP
William R. Cox

The Eggerleys weren't very smart. They trained their sights on Will Carney and Arizona's biggest blood bath began.

THE DEPUTY OF SAN RIANO
Lawrence A. Keating and
Al. P. Nelson

When a man fell dead from his horse, Ed Grant was spotted riding away from the scene. The deputy sheriff rode out after him and came up against everything from gunfire to dynamite.

FARGO: MASSACRE RIVER
John Benteen

The ambushers up ahead had now blocked the road. Fargo's convoy was a jumble, a perfect target for the insurgents' weapons!

SUNDANCE: DEATH IN THE LAVA
John Benteen

The Modoc's captured the wagon train and its cargo of gold. But now the halfbreed they called Sundance was going after it . . .

HARSH RECKONING
Phil Ketchum

Five years of keeping himself alive in a brutal prison had made Brand tough and careless about who he gunned down . . .

FARGO: PANAMA GOLD
John Benteen

With foreign money behind him, Buckner was going to destroy the Panama Canal before it could be completed. Fargo's job was to stop Buckner.

FARGO:
THE SHARPSHOOTERS
John Benteen

The Canfield clan, thirty strong were raising hell in Texas. Fargo was tough enough to hold his own against the whole clan.

PISTOL LAW
Paul Evan Lehman

Lance Jones came back to Mustang for just one thing — revenge! Revenge on the people who had him thrown in jail.

HELL RIDERS
Steve Mensing

Wade Walker's kid brother, Duane, was locked up in the Silver City jail facing a rope at dawn. Wade was a ruthless outlaw, but he was smart, and he had vowed to have his brother out of jail before morning!

DESERT OF THE DAMNED
Nelson Nye

The law was after him for the murder of a marshal — a murder he didn't commit. Breen was after him for revenge — and Breen wouldn't stop at anything . . . blackmail, a frameup . . . or murder.

DAY OF THE COMANCHEROS
Steven C. Lawrence

Their very name struck terror into men's hearts — the Comancheros, a savage army of cutthroats who swept across Texas, leaving behind a bloodstained trail of robbery and murder.

SUNDANCE: SILENT ENEMY
John Benteen

A lone crazed Cheyenne was on a personal war path. They needed to pit one man against one crazed Indian. That man was Sundance.

LASSITER
Jack Slade

Lassiter wasn't the kind of man to listen to reason. Cross him once and he'll hold a grudge for years to come — if he let you live that long.

LAST STAGE TO GOMORRAH
Barry Cord

Jeff Carter, tough ex-riverboat gambler, now had himself a horse ranch that kept him free from gunfights and card games. Until Sturvesant of Wells Fargo showed up.

McALLISTER ON THE COMANCHE CROSSING
Matt Chisholm

The Comanche, McAllister owes them a life — and the trail is soaked with the blood of the men who had tried to outrun them before.

QUICK-TRIGGER COUNTRY
Clem Colt

Turkey Red hooked up with Curly Bill Graham's outlaw crew. But wholesale murder was out of Turk's line, so when range war flared he bucked the whole border gang alone . . .

CAMPAIGNING
Jim Miller

Ambushed on the Santa Fe trail, Sean Callahan is saved by two Indian strangers. But there'll be more lead and arrows flying before the band join Kit Carson against the Comanches.

GUNSLINGER'S RANGE
Jackson Cole

Three escaped convicts are out for revenge. They won't rest until they put a bullet through the head of the dirty snake who locked them behind bars.

RUSTLER'S TRAIL
Lee Floren

Jim Carlin knew he would have to stand up and fight because he had staked his claim right in the middle of Big Ike Outland's best grass.

THE TRUTH ABOUT SNAKE RIDGE
Marshall Grover

The troubleshooters came to San Cristobal to help the needy. For Larry and Stretch the turmoil began with a brawl and then an ambush.

WOLF DOG RANGE
Lee Floren

Will Ardery would stop at nothing, unless something stopped him first — like a bullet from Pete Manly's gun.

DEVIL'S DINERO
Marshall Grover

Plagued by remorse, a rich old reprobate hired the Texas Troubleshooters to deliver a fortune in greenbacks to each of his victims.

GUNS OF FURY
Ernest Haycox

Dane Starr, alias Dan Smith, wanted to close the door on his past and hang up his guns, but people wouldn't let him.

DONOVAN
Elmer Kelton

Donovan was supposed to be dead. Uncle Joe Vickers had fired off both barrels of a shotgun into the vicious outlaw's face as he was escaping from jail. Now Uncle Joe had been shot — in just the same way.

CODE OF THE GUN
Gordon D. Shirreffs

MacLean came riding home, with saddle tramp written all over him, but sewn in his shirt-lining was an Arizona Ranger's star.

GAMBLER'S GUN LUCK
Brett Austen

Gamblers seldom live long. Parker was a hell of a gambler. It was his life — or his death . . .

ORPHAN'S PREFERRED
Jim Miller

Sean Callahan answers the call of the Pony Express and fights Indians and outlaws to get the mail through.

DAY OF THE BUZZARD
T. V. Olsen

All Val Penmark cared about was getting the men who killed his wife.

THE MANHUNTER
Gordon D. Shirreffs

Lee Kershaw knew that every Rurale in the territory was on the lookout for him. But the offer of $5,000 in gold to find five small pieces of leather was too good to turn down.

RIFLES ON THE RANGE
Lee Floren

Doc Mike and the farmer stood there alone between Smith and Watson. There was this moment of stillness, and then the roar would start. And somebody would die . . .

HARTIGAN
Marshall Grover

Hartigan had come to Cornerstone to die. He chose the time and the place, and Main Street became a battlefield.

SUNDANCE: OVERKILL
John Benteen

When a wealthy banker's daughter was kidnapped by the Cheyenne, he offered Sundance $10,000 to rescue the girl.